Did he have to have his pound of flesh, too?

"Beth. Don't." His voice was raw, and before she knew what was happening his arms were around her, dragging her close into his body, and for one insane moment she allowed herself to melt, to cling to him, blocking his mind to the way things were.

"Tell me what's wrong," Charles whispered darkly, one strong hand cradling her head against a solid angle of his shoulder, and the blood began to beat thickly through her veins, drugging her, and only when his other hand began a slow caressing movement along the length of her spine did she realize what she was doing.

"Leave me alone, can't you?"

"Why the hell should I? You're still my wife, damn it!"

DIANA HAMILTON is a true romantic and fell in love with her husband at first sight. They still live in the fairy-tale Tudor house where they raised their three children. Now the idyll is shared with eight rescued cats and a puppy. But despite an often chaotic life-style, Diana has always had her nose in a book—either reading or writing one!

Books by Diana Hamilton

HARLEQUIN PRESENTS

HARLEQUIN ROMANCE

DIANA HAMILTON

Savage Obsession

Harlequin Books

TORONTO • NEW YORK • LONDON
AMSTERDAM • PARIS • SYDNEY • HAMBURG
STOCKHOLM • ATHENS • TOKYO • MILAN
MADRID • WARSAW • BUDAPEST • AUCKLAND

Harlequin Presents first edition September 1993
ISBN 0-373-11588-1

Original hardcover edition published in 1992
by Mills & Boon Limited

SAVAGE OBSESSION

CHAPTER ONE

SHE should never have married him. She'd been such a fool to even consider the possibility that it could work. Such a damned fool!

Beth's small fists beat uselessly against the broad window-ledge and a sudden hot spurt of tears blurred the view of South Park's magnificent gardens. Clamping her teeth together, she turned from the window and back into the body of her bedroom. No time to weep, no time to begin the battle to overcome the shock that left her coldly aching inside, no time to try to come to terms with what she had seen, what she had heard.

So maybe tonight's dinner party was a blessing in disguise, she informed herself drily. Acting the part of the woman Charles Savage had married— the perfect hostess to his business colleagues, people who could be useful to him—would help her to ride the pain.

But she knew that small, frigid consolation was nothing but a chimera when she met the mute misery in her reflected green eyes. How could she begin to come to terms with the knowledge that Zanna Hall, the woman who had been the obsessive love of Charles's life, was here again? Obviously at his invitation, and, what was worse, so much worse, complete with their illegitimate two-year-old son, the fruit of their passionate, ill-fated affair!

For a moment the shocking intensity of the pain she had kept under control since her miscarriage three months ago threatened to pull her slender frame apart, but she conquered it, denied it, before it reached the intolerable level that would leave her useless, fit for nothing.

Compressing the sweet curve of her mouth, she lifted a comb, frowning at the slight tremor of her hand, and dragged it through her straight dark hair, setting the elegant bob to rights. She would do what she always did at this time when they were entertaining. Stick rigidly to routine, that way she might be safe, come through the advancing ordeal with her dignity intact.

Dignity, or at least the show of it, was all she had. She certainly had no pride or self-respect to hold on to. She never had had, not where Charles was concerned. Couldn't have done, or she never would have agreed to marry him.

Deliberately closing her eyes to that degrading piece of self-knowledge, she walked briskly out of the room and made her way to the kitchens. Check with Mrs Penny on progress in the kitchen. Their guests would begin to arrive at any moment now. Rooms were ready. Business discussions would go on through most of the weekend. Two wives tagging along this time, needing to be entertained tomorrow while the men were incommunicado. Gentle tours of South Park's gardens always went well, especially so in this glorious June weather. Tea on the terrace, idle female chit-chat, maybe a drive down to the village in the morning to look at the Norman church, the picturesque remains of the abbey.

And never a hint of what she was going through, what she was feeling.

Entering the enormous kitchen, Beth was greeted by the scent of freshly chopped herbs and Mrs Penny, who had been cook-cum-housekeeper at South Park—apart from one brief and fateful absence three years ago—since Charles's parents had lived here, said grumpily,

'As if there isn't enough to do!' She was doing something unnecessarily vigorous with a fish kettle and her small shrewd blue eyes were snapping as she glanced sideways up at Beth. 'You do know, ducky, as how that madam is back? Walked in as large as life demanding tea to be sent to the study, milk and biscuits for the nipper. Dead spit he is, too. Shameless, I call it.'

Rigidly, Beth turned to inspect the freshly prepared vegetables put ready on the butcher's block. So Mrs Penny had picked up the unmistakable likeness between father and son. It was, after all, quite unmissable.

Trying to will the stiffness out of her neck and shoulders, she fastened her eyes on the various pans. No point in advertising her misery and humiliation. Fresh peas, courgettes, tiny potatoes and baby broad beans, all picked from South Park's walled vegetable garden early this morning, but her interest was feigned, doing nothing at all to block out Mrs Penny's relentless tirade.

'And when I went to collect the tray, not ten minutes ago, she was still there and telling me, if you please, how she'd come to stay. "I'd like you to prepare a room for me, Mrs Penny," she said— all bossy, like, "and one for Harry, of course."

That's the nipper. Nice little lad, he looked, and it's not his fault, is it? Can't hold that against him, poor brat. And I told her straight, I did. "I'm afraid as how I'm much too busy, Miss Hall. It is still Miss Hall, isn't it?'' And she never contradicted, said oh, no, she'd gone and married Tom or Dick— or Harry's dad!' As if to emphasise her extreme busyness, she stamped to the sink and turned the tap on a head of lettuce. Shouting above the gush of water, she declared, 'I can't think what that man of yours is about, giving her houseroom, that I can't! She's been nothing but trouble, that I do know!'

Beth knew perfectly well why Charles was giving Zanna houseroom, but it was something she couldn't bear to think of right now so she replied repressively, with unconscious and ironical truth, 'I'm sure Mr Savage has his reasons.'

And Mrs Penny snorted irrepressibly,

'Don't you "Mr Savage" me, ducky! Charlie-boy it's always been, since I first came to work for his folks when he was ten years old. And Charlie-boy it always will be!'

Beth shuddered. She wished she had Mrs Penny's confidence, her sense of belonging—come what may. At one time, blessed with the power of love, with the blind hope of youth, she had possessed all that. Possessed the determination to force her darling Charles into loving her, truly loving her, sure that, given time, he would forget that wild, turbulent, ill-fated passion that had been his obsessive love for Zanna Hall.

Fool.

Forcing a smile, she said as lightly as she could, 'If everything's under control, I'll go and wait for the first of our guests. It's late enough to forget about tea. Charles will offer drinks. I'll go and root him out.'

But she didn't. Of course she didn't. She had been on her way to do just that, guessing he'd be in his study because, half an hour before, as she'd been putting the final touches to the dinner table, she'd heard his car.

Nowadays, he no longer bothered to announce his arrival. Their marriage had degenerated into a distant thing, both coolly polite on the surface because anything else would have been unthinkable, but withdrawing from each other, the tide of their relationship inexorably ebbing.

Approaching the study, she'd painted the tiny, impersonal smile on her face, almost habitual now because she'd promised herself that she would never allow him to see just how much pain and distress his physical and mental movement away from her gave. For him to even guess at the passionate love she still bore him would be unproductive, would probably dismay and disgust him into retreating still further from the rocky shores of their marriage. She'd grown into the habit of biding her time, waiting, hoping, being all that he needed her to be and no more. Never anything more. Not now.

The study door had been ajar, just a little, and her hand had been upraised to push against the smooth wood when that husky, horribly remembered voice had stopped her in her tracks. She would never forget Zanna's siren tones. Not even if she lived to be a hundred. And at first it hadn't made sense; nightmares rarely did, did they? Because Zanna had broken away three years ago, or nearly, leaving Charles devastated, living in brooding isolation at South Park, a meaty subject for gossiping village tongues. So she couldn't have returned, could she? She couldn't be saying,

'I had to come to you again, darling. That ill-begotten marriage is finished now. Over. And I won't pretend I'm not glad—I can't be that much of a hypocrite. Besides, our son needs to get to know his father, you won't deny that. As a single parent I've given Harry all the love in the world, but he still needs his father.'

Instinctively, Beth's hand had eased the door open, just a little, the reflection of puzzled disbelief in her deep green eyes changing to shock as they took in the picture that would be printed on her retinas for all time.

Zanna, as flamboyantly lovely as ever, her red-gold hair curling bewitchingly around her heart-stopping features, Charles, hovering above her as she lounged back in one of the leather-covered armchairs, the stern, hard features softened to an expression that Beth hadn't seen for months. Was never likely to see again outside of tormenting dreams. And the child.

Around two years old. Playing on the floor with a paperweight in his chubby little hands, banging the smooth glass temporary toy gleefully down on the thick carpet, oblivious to the vibrations that were making the air above his innocent head hum. Oblivious of his true parentage, for now. Of the remarkable family resemblance, the raven hue of that silky hair, the deep, deep grey of the black-fringed eyes, the cast of the features that would, in time, be an almost mirror-image of the man whose eyes were now fastened on him with all too naked longing.

Slipping away, unseen and unheard, she had made it to her bathroom in time to part with her lunch and had then forced herself to confront the unbelievable, the shock and pain of knowing that Zanna was back, complete with the son Charles had longed for.

Following the break-up of his tempestuous relationship with Zanna, Charles had married her, Beth, not exactly on the rebound but with a cool calculation that had almost taken her breath away.

He had wanted a wife, a child to inherit—several children, in point of fact. And she, Beth, was suitable, had proved herself capable, in Mrs Penny's absence, of running South Park like clockwork and, as an added bonus, acting as his hostess when he entertained business contacts, stepping into the shoes Zanna had vacated.

His proposal had hit her like a bomb, and she had been suffering from shell-shock when she'd accepted, must have been to have ignored the well-meaning advice of her parents and Allie, her best friend and business partner. But still sufficiently in control of her wits to keep him in ignorance of the way she felt about him.

A man of his urbane sophistication, possessing the drive and ambition that had wrested the family-owned communications business out of the undistinguished dust of failure and planted it firmly back on its feet, would have thought her a fool of the first water if she'd leapt into his arms and confessed that she'd loved him from afar ever since she'd been a starry-eyed teenager! That most of the village girls had yearned over the darkly brooding good looks of Charles Savage of South Park, the unattainable, the impossibly sexy Charles. That those other girls had grown out of the state of infatuation, had found real, attainable men-friends, but that she, Beth Garner, had done no such thing, had loved him always, could see no end to that love.

The arrival of the first of the weekend guests had Beth thrusting her misery to the back of her mind, and, as if by telepathy, Charles was there, by her side, no hint in his steely gunfighter's eyes of the emotion he must have felt when he met his son for the very first time.

Or had it been for the first time? she wondered tormentedly as he smiled at her over the head of one of the visiting wives, the slight curve of his mouth doing nothing to bring warmth to those narrow, steely grey eyes, but doing everything to bring that bitter-sweet stabbing pain to the pit of her stomach.

This overriding sexual awareness of him was something she was going to have to school out of existence, she recognised with a hopeless anguish that was down to the fact that she had been trying to accomplish just that ever since he had made it plain that he was no longer interested in the physical side of their marriage.

She saw him suddenly frown, those smokily unreadable eyes probing hers, and she said quickly, far too brightly, 'Why don't I show you to your room, Mavis? I just know Charles is about to offer Donald a drink, and——'

'I rather think they'd both appreciate the chance to freshen up,' Charles cut in smoothly, lifting the two pieces of expensive luggage and ushering his guests towards the stairs, tossing back over his shoulder, 'The others should be here at any moment, they're arriving together. Wait, would you, darling?'

No, thanks, Beth thought sickly as his tall, leanly supple body disappeared round the bend in the staircase. He probably wanted to break the news of the arrival of the principle guests—his former lover and their son—in private. It wouldn't be the type of information he would want to impart in front of a houseful of business associates!

Well, that was his problem. She mounted the stairs quickly, intent on gaining the privacy of her own room. As far as Charles was aware, she didn't know Zanna and Harry were here. And, stupidly, she had the craziest feeling that until he actually spoke of their presence she didn't really have to face up to it.

It was something too awful to be faced, she thought jaggedly as she neared the head of the stairs, trying to ignore the knowledge that Charles must have contacted Zanna, told her that his ill-considered marriage to little Beth Garner had irretrievably broken down. Was over. Finished. The conversation she had overheard had made that much clear.

Had he pleaded with his former lover? Confessed he hadn't been able to get her out of his system?

Unwanted questions prodded at her mind, like a
tongue probing an aching tooth, increasing the pain,
her head awash with unwelcome conjectures as she
took the corridor that led away from the guest wing
and down to her own room.

And what had been Zanna's reaction? Easy. No
problem in working that one out. She'd probably
regretted the break-up as much as he had, her pride
keeping her away until it had been too late to do
anything about it because by the time she had discovered she was expecting his child he had married
his temporary housekeeper!

And having disappeared from the scene she'd
kept well away from it. No real problem there,
either. The pampered only child of wealthy parents,
she and her baby would have been well taken care
of. She had probably spent the last two and a half
years with them at their villa in the south of France
where her parents had repaired to spend their early
retirement.

But she was back on the scene now, with a vengeance, and no, Charles couldn't have known of
Harry's existence until he'd contacted her, ex-
plaining that as far as he was concerned his marriage was over. Nothing on earth would have kept
his son from him, had he known. And nothing on
earth would keep him from him now. Just as
nothing would keep him apart from the only woman
he had ever loved.

She was shaking all over as she reached her room
and, childlike, she bunched her hands into fists and
knuckled them to her mouth, biting down on the
whitened skin, welcoming the distraction of physical
pain. Somehow, somehow, she had to keep a hold

on herself, ride out the storm until Sunday afternoon when the weekend guests would leave. And just behind her Charles reminded coldly,

'I asked you to remain downstairs.'

He hadn't set foot inside this room since her miscarriage three months ago, had kept severely to the room they had once shared, the master bedroom, and his intrusion here, now, under these circumstances, was a violation of her space, her privacy, and the only way to combat an incipient breakdown was to keep her head, her dignity, to somehow fight fire with fire.

So she shrugged, just a little, maintaining a veneer of cool collectedness at enormous cost to her mental equilibrium.

'I'm quite sure you're perfectly able to greet your guests and settle them in.' Her voice, in her own ears, sounded strangely brittle. 'It's time I showered and changed.'

She forced herself to turn and face him then, her head rigidly high, her tongue feeling dry, too large for her mouth, as she dragged the words out, 'If I'm to make myself presentable, dispense drinks and small talk to your guests, and help Mrs Penny with the final touches to dinner—she can't make a successful mayonnaise no matter how hard she tries, bless her—then I don't have time to hang around waiting for late-comers. We don't want anything to upset the routine and ruin the weekend, do we?'

It was the longest speech she'd made to him in ages, and there was a warning there, if he cared to look for it. She would go to pieces when he told her he wanted a divorce, that he wanted to marry Zanna, the only woman he was capable of loving, to marry her and claim his son. And she would rather not have that happen until the weekend was over, their guests safely out of the house.

Just for a moment she thought she saw a flash of anger deep in the unrevealing smoke-grey eyes, but then it was gone, or perhaps it had never been, she decided as his habitually bland expression gazed straight back at her.

Her eyes dropped, the contact was too painful, and when she found herself hungrily watching his long, very beautifully sculpted mouth she dragged in a raspingly painful breath and turned away, walking over towards the generous hanging cupboard, making a show of sorting through the garments for something to wear.

The best way to rid herself of his presence was to begin to undress, ready for her shower, she informed herself cynically. He hadn't wanted to look at her, to touch her, in months. She hadn't known why, not until now.

Almost defiantly, she kicked off her shoes, lifting her hands to the buttons of her light cotton blouse, but her desperate ploy didn't work because he said tonelessly, 'Zanna Hall is here,' and Beth froze, her back to him, her heart pounding because this was crunch time. He was going to tell her something she didn't think she was strong enough to hear, and he went on levelly, his deep rough-velvet voice under strict control, 'With her son. Harry is two years old. They will be staying for a few days.'

'Oh, really.' If she sounded uninterested she couldn't help it. To pretend indifference was the only way she would be able to handle this.

In retrospect, she was thankful that he had never told her he loved her, said those words she would have given anything in the world to hear, the words that would have opened the dam of her own deep love for him, had her confessing the abiding strength of her passion. Had she been fool enough, unguarded enough, to do so then this weekend would have been even more humiliating, more degrading—if that were possible.

'Aren't you going to ask why?'

He had moved. She could tell by his voice that he was standing much closer now and she shivered, biting out, 'No,' tightly, very quickly, because she already knew why Zanna was here, with Charles's son; she didn't need him to spell it out.

Blindly, she dragged the first garment to come to hand out of the cupboard, still with her back to him because she couldn't bear to see the final rejection in his magnificent eyes when he told her that he no longer wanted her as his wife.

He swore then, softly, almost inaudibly, and, clutching the dress close to her chest like a piece of armour, she heard him say, the first intimation of strain in his voice, 'For some reason best known to herself, Mrs Penny refused to make a room ready for Zanna and young Harry.' Attuned to every last thing about him, she heard the softening of his tone as he mentioned the child. His child. The son he had wanted. The son she had been unable to give him. And he was going to ask her to do it, to make time to settle them in, make them comfortable. It was unbelievable! And she was proved right when he went on, a rare and raw emotion colouring his voice, 'I wonder if you'd mind——?'

'I've already said I'm pushed for time.' She was ready for him; she'd learned that particular trick ever since she'd made herself face the fact of his growing distaste for her. A useful defence mechanism. 'You invited them here, apparently. You find them somewhere to sleep—I don't care where. It's up to you.' And walked rapidly, rigidly, like a jerky puppet, across the bedroom floor towards the door of her bathroom, still clutching the dress in front of her.

Her voice had emerged coolly, and she didn't know how it could have done because there was a scream building up inside her and her heart was pattering hysterically beneath her breast, and she slammed the bathroom door behind her, ramming the bolt home, leaning against the smooth dark wood.

Not that Charles would have attempted to follow her, of course. He had lost what interest he'd ever had in her when she had miscarried their child. Nowadays they treated each other like strangers— only this evening had he broken the habit of distance that had been deepening ever since that dreadful night three months ago. And no prizes for guessing why, she thought on a flare of anger, dragging her clothes off with shaking hands.

'Are you all right?'

The last thing she had expected was this rare show of compassion, a softening of the austerely crafted, remote features. But then, she thought, side-stepping him, her hands tightening on the coffee-tray, he was probably sorry for her. His pity was the last thing she wanted.

'I'm fine. Shouldn't I be?' she challenged, then regretted the impulse because she didn't want to give him the opportunity to tell her exactly why she should be feeling so very far from 'all right'. Dinner had been an ordeal she would rather forget, with Zanna's vibrant beauty, her easy wit, making her the centre of attention. And heaven only knew what had been going on inside the Clarkes' heads! Donald Clarke had been Charles's company accountant for years, right through the time of his tempestuous affair with Zanna. She had lived here at South Park in those days, on and off, had acted as his hostess at many a weekend such as this. Donald and Mavis would be dying to retreat to the privacy of their room to chew over the scandal of Zanna's return. And they could hardly have forgotten the wild obsession of Charles's love-affair with the woman who, even then, had left a string of broken hearts in her wake, or forgotten his brooding desolation when she had finally walked out on him, too.

'I thought you might have had one of your headaches,' Charles said, a thread of tension running through the expressed concern. 'You have that pallid look about you.'

As he took the tray from her and waited for her to precede him through the kitchen door she muttered, 'Thanks!' meaning his unflattering description, and nothing to do with the way he'd appeared to help her with the unwieldy tray. True, since the road accident that had resulted in the loss of their child, she had suffered from violent headaches, a legacy not only from the concussion, but from grief. But did he really have to draw her at-

tention to the fact that beside the glowingly vibrant
beauty of his former lover, the mother of his child,
she looked like a sadly anaemic mouse?

'If you'd like to call it a day, I'll make your excuses,' he offered as they walked through the vast
hall together, and she glanced up at him quickly,
suspicion narrowing her glittering green eyes. But
instead of the suspected sarcasm, a desire to be rid
of her, see her tucked up in bed and safely out of
the way, she saw only compassion. And she looked
away quickly, hot tears in her eyes. She had known
she was losing him long before now, had tried to
deny it, to hang on to hope, but his action in
bringing Zanna here, and their son, meant that all
hope was gone.

And he was standing too close, the tautly muscled
length of him, his breadth of shoulder, the sexy
narrowness of hips moulded by the fine dark suiting
making the muscles around her heart clench with
pain, and when she caught her breath on a strangled
sob he put the tray down on one of the tables set
against the panelled wall and cupped her face in
his hands, the narrowed eyes dark with sympathy,
his mouth tight as he told her, 'I'm so sorry, Beth.
The last thing I ever intended to do was cause you
pain.'

And at that moment she believed him. His obsession with Zanna had been legendary, and it still
lived. He probably didn't want it to, but it did.
There was nothing he could do about it, and the
existence of their child made her impossible to
resist.

Beth made a huge effort to control herself,
fighting the almost irresistible impulse to lay her

head against his chest and weep for the love she had lost without ever having it. If he knew just how much she was breaking up inside he would pity her even more. And that she simply could not stand. So she said thinly, jerking her head away as if his touch, instead of making her yearning for him unbearable, in fact disgusted her,

'I'll believe you—thousands wouldn't!' And he could make what he liked of that, anything, just as long as he never learned the truth—that she loved him so much she would die for him if she had to. 'I think I will go to bed.' She swung on her heels, not looking at him. 'I'd be grateful if you would make my apologies.'

Needless to say, she didn't sleep, didn't even try to. She stared the ruins of her marriage in the face as the light faded from the sky at the end of the glorious June day, alternatively loving and hating him.

The love had begun as an infatuation. She'd been fifteen and yearning over the sexy Charles Savage had been quite the fashion for the village girls. Recently down from Oxford with a first-class degree, he'd driven fast cars and brought a new girlfriend home every weekend, or so it had seemed. His mother had been dead for many years at that time, his father losing his grip on reality. His younger brother, James, had been around then, too. But he'd refused to have anything to do with the ailing family business, leaving it to Charles to knuckle down and retrieve the fortunes of the family at South Park.

Staring from her lonely window at the purple dusk, Beth wondered what had happened to James.

The last she'd heard, through Charles, had been the news of the death of James's wife, Lisa. Somewhere abroad. She should have made it her business to find out more, to write to him, expressing her sympathy. She had never met Lisa; she and James had not even attended hers and Charles's wedding two years ago. There had been a rift between the brothers, that much she had known, although Charles had always refused to talk about the younger man. And, at the time, she excused herself—she had been suffering badly from the miscarriage of her child. Nevertheless, she should have made some effort to express her sympathy...

She sighed. She didn't know why now, of all times, she should be thinking of James. Except that, remembering earlier times, when she'd first fallen in love with the unattainable Charles Savage, she could recall one incident with utmost clarity.

It would have been around five years ago. She and her bosom friend, Alison, had just started up in business on their own, but they'd made time to go to the May Day hop in the village hall. Charles and James had put in an appearance, as they usually did, and of course, by that time, Beth's contemporaries had got over their collective infatuation for the heir to South Park, were going steady with more prosaic, yet attainable local boys.

But not Beth, of course. What had begun as a fashionable schoolgirl crush had, annoyingly, grown into love. Not that she'd confided in anyone, of course. Not even Allie. It was a secret she'd kept to herself—as if it were a pernicious vice—only James, it seemed, guessing the truth.

That was the first time she'd seen Zanna. She'd swept into the village hall on Charles's arm, looking like a rare hot-house orchid in a field of common daisies, and James had followed, a pale carbon of his devastating brother, his features sulky. And later, sweeping her round the floor in a duty dance, James had told her,

'You never did stand much of a chance; Charles was always attracted by the rarer species. But this time he's cast his net and captured the incomparable Zanna Hall, so you, my dear little sparrow, won't get a look-in.'

At the time, she'd been too mortified by the way he'd guessed the truth about her to say a word. Besides, from the way Charles looked at the newest lady in his life, he was clearly besotted. And she wondered now if James had resented his brother's easy conquest of the most delectable females around, and if that lay behind the rift. In any case, shortly after that, James had married. He'd been working abroad at the time, as a civil engineer, and as far as she knew he'd never brought Lisa to South Park.

She wondered, fleetingly, if he had been surprised when his brother had married the insignificant Beth Garner and knew he wouldn't be surprised at all to learn how the marriage had broken up. His long-ago words at the May Day dance had been prophetic.

She woke feeling grim. She had fallen asleep on the wide window-ledge and she stumbled to her feet, her movements ungainly. Feeling her way around the furniture, she located the light switch and banished the darkness.

If only she could banish the darkness within, she thought despairingly, looking at her smooth, lonely bed and knowing she would never get to sleep until something had been sorted out.

One way or another.

Contrary to her earlier, shock-numbed instincts, she knew she couldn't get through the night, the rest of the interminable weekend, without talking this through with Charles.

It would take courage to go to the room he had thrown her out of after her illness. But she could manage it. She had to.

He had taken her to the master bedroom when she'd first entered South Park as his bride; it was there she had known those nights of ecstasy, the immature hope that one day, sooner or later, he would grow to love her as she loved him. There that their child had been conceived.

But, returning from hospital, she had found that her things had been moved to the room she now occupied, and he'd explained that he thought it best if they slept apart until she was fully recovered. Not that he'd been unkind about it, she thought with a tiny shudder. He'd never been unkind, ever; he'd been a considerate, warm, appreciative—if demanding—husband. Even after the accident and her miscarriage, when any affection he'd felt for her had died along with the child they had lost, he had still treated her with respect and politeness.

Which made his cruelty in bringing Zanna and their son here all the more devastating.

Yet he wasn't a cruel man. Self-assured, fairly ruthless in his business dealings, frustratingly enigmatic at times and sometimes impossible, he was all of these things. But never deliberately cruel.

Clinging to that knowledge, she tightened the belt of her silky robe and left her room, her soft mouth set with grim determination. She wasn't going to stand meekly by and watch her life and her marriage fall apart without trying to do something about it.

That Charles would choose to stay with her, having never loved her, particularly since, following the accident and the miscarriage, she had been told she might never conceive again, when he could have the woman who had once dominated his life, and the child they had created together, was a pretty forlorn hope, but she was an optimist, wasn't she? She had to be, to have agreed to marry him in the first place!

But even that failed her as she reached the corner where the corridor turned to lead to the master bedroom suite. With the influx of house guests, all the rooms were occupied, so where else would Zanna sleep, except in his bed?

Walking into that sumptuous room and finding them tangled together in the huge bed was something she simply couldn't face, and the determination that had brought her this far drained out of her, leaving her limp and shaking, leaning against the wall for support, her heartbeats frantic.

But finding them together would settle the thing once and for all, wouldn't it? she told herself tiredly. She couldn't go through the remainder of the weekend not knowing what was going on, not knowing for sure. She was out of shock now, and had to know.

Pulling away from the wall, she walked doggedly on down the dimly lit corridor then gasped with anguish as she saw the glimmer of a night-light from the partly open door of the nursery.

Charles and Zanna had put their child in the room she had so lovingly created for her baby! She didn't know how much more she could endure! Yet, driven by a need she couldn't put a name to, she silently approached the open door, moving like a sleep-walker.

And through the gap she saw them. The sleeping child, the parents looking down on him. Charles, his dark hair rumpled, his towelling robe revealing long, tautly muscled, hair-roughened legs, his arm around Zanna's naked shoulders—naked except for the narrow shoestring straps which supported her clinging satin nightdress—and he was saying softly,

'Don't worry about it. Everything's going to work out. There isn't a man alive who wouldn't welcome that child into his family. And I'm no exception.'

CHAPTER TWO

'So WHAT'S happened?' Allie wanted to know, her round face very serious. And Beth turned from the stance she had taken up at the sash window, looking down on the deserted Sunday-afternoon high street of the market town and replied evenly,

'Nothing's happened. I feel like getting back to work. Lots of married women do it.' That was her story, and she was sticking to it. Best friend or not, she couldn't confide in Allie; she would, and quite truthfully, say 'I told you so!'

'If you say so,' the other girl said slowly, stringing the words out, then jumped up from the sofa, her smile brisk now. 'I'll make a drink, then we can see what's on the books. Tea or coffee?'

'Oh... Tea, please.' Beth tugged herself together—she'd been miles away, wondering how she was going to come to terms with life without Charles, and caught the quick upward jerk of her friend's brows and warned herself to be more careful.

Watching Allie walk through to the kitchen of the small flat above the agency office, Beth pulled in a deep breath, exhaling it slowly. So far she'd done well. The struggle back to self-respect had begun and she deserved to feel proud of herself.

As soon as the last of the weekend guests had departed earlier that afternoon she had made up her mind to drive over to see Allie. She hadn't driven since the accident. Charles had been behind the wheel on that terrible day when a drunken youth had overtaken on a blind bend and had caused the accident that had cost her the life of her unborn child.

There hadn't been a thing Charles could have done to avoid it, and the fact that he had emerged with minor cuts and abrasions, while she had landed in hospital with a severe concussion, several broken ribs and a dangerous miscarriage, had been the luck of the draw.

So today nerving herself to take her car out had been the second positive step back on the road to the recovery of her self-respect.

And the first had come when Charles had turned to her after they'd speeded the last of the departing house guests on their way, telling her quietly but with a firmness that brooked no argument, 'Come to the study, Beth. Zanna and I have something to tell you.' He turned back towards the house, sunlight glinting on his raven-dark hair, highlighting the harsh, angular planes of his face, and if there was any expression in those narrowed smoky-grey eyes she couldn't read it.

But this time she was arguing, fighting her corner, and she had tossed back at him levelly, 'Sorry. I've an appointment. Whatever you have to tell me will have to wait.' Wait until she had sorted out the next few weeks of her life, could present her husband with a *fait accompli*. She knew damn well what he and Zanna had to tell her and she needed to get her say in first. There were winners and losers in every game but she was determined to make sure that, as far as appearances went, she didn't come out of this hateful mess in second place.

Ignoring the sudden angry line of his mouth, she had stridden away, her feet crunching on the gravel as she made for the garages. From deep inside the house she had caught the sound of childish, gurgling laughter and she'd had to fight hard to control the insane impulse to hurl herself into Charles's arms and beg him not to leave her.

Aware of those brooding grey eyes on her back, she had forced herself on, her head high, telling herself that, despite her other shortcomings, Zanna was a good mother. Throughout the last dreadful two days she had observed the care the other woman lavished on the child and Beth had to rub that fact in, that and every other known piece of information, rub it in until it hurt, because that was the only way she could prevent herself from begging Charles to stay with her.

And the deeper the pain the more likely she was to regain the pride she had thrown away when she had agreed to be his wife, she had assured herself, steeling every nerve and muscle to open the door of the Metro Charles had provided her with shortly after their marriage, the car she hadn't had the guts to drive since the accident.

'Are you saying you want to come back into partnership?' Allie asked now, returning with two mugs of tea, and Beth shook her head, making herself smile as she took one of them and sank down on the sofa.

'Not necessarily.' The Helpline Agency, which they'd started together, was run from here, not ten

miles away from South Park, and Beth didn't want
to be this close.

Working locally, she wouldn't be able to avoid
seeing Charles and Zanna and their son from time
to time. Besides, her parents still lived in the village
although her father had retired from medical
practice a year ago, and they would expect her to
visit them regularly, and every time she did she
would have to drive right past the impressive gates
of the South Park estate.

'Well, I can't see the lord of the manor allowing
his wife to scrub floors, clean offices, cook for
private dinner parties or dance attendance on a
senile old lady,' Allie grinned, flicking through a
much thumbed leather-bound book. 'Though
you're not qualified for nursing duties, of course.
And I can't see——'

'Anything in the secretarial line? That I am
qualified for,' Beth put in, hoping she didn't sound
too desperate. She needed to earn her living, be independent, and a part-time post, which was what
the agency specialised in, would tide her over until
she could find something permanent, as far away
from here as was possible to get.

'Sorry.' Allie wrinkled her nose. 'Plenty last
week, but nothing this. There's only one, and that's
not suitable.'

'Pity.' Beth took a sip of scalding tea, trying to
hide her deep disappointment. Nothing was ever
easy, and walking straight into a job as she had
hoped was, apparently, not on. She would have to
get right away and look for permanent work. Not
so simple. She could take the car, of course, since
it had been a birthday gift, but she wouldn't, on

principle, touch a penny of the generous allowance Charles paid into her private account. Finding affordable accommodation while she looked for work could be a headache.

And because Allie was astute, highly adept at picking up vibrations, Beth decided she had to show an interest, and she managed idly, 'So what's so unsuitable about the only position you appear to be unable to fill?' and had to force herself to keep her cool when Allie dismissed,

'It's in France. An English writer living in Boulogne—he moved there years ago, apparently, buying and renovating a small farmhouse a few kilometres inland.' Allie bit unrepentently into her third chocolate biscuit and said through a mouthful of crumbs, 'It sounds a peach of a job. His permanent English secretary did a runner with a German hunk she met at Le Touquet and left him stranded. He wants a temp to take over while he hunts for another permanent lady—someone on the wrong side of fifty, and prim with it, so he says!' She tapped the open book in front of her reflectively. 'Betty Mayhew—you remember her, of course—is dead keen. And if he's still unsuited by the time she finishes her stint with Comtech, she can have a stab at it.'

'Betty was always good at getting what she wanted,' Beth reminded Allie smoothly, recalling the vibrantly attractive blonde who seemed to sail through life, and men-friends, with insouciant ease. She had been one of the first secretaries she and Allie had signed up all that time ago, and if she'd set her sights on a spell in north-west France then, for once, she was going to be disappointed.

Bitchy! she scolded herself tartly, then added decisively, 'Pity to miss out with a new client. I'll go. And don't think I've lost all my skills,' she admonished, deliberately misinterpreting her friend's pole-axed stare. 'I've done a fair bit of work for Charles, off and on; I've kept up to date, believe me.'

'Oh, I do,' Allie came right back. 'I do. But will Charles mind having an absentee wife? And don't think he can come up with something flash and buy a helicopter to ferry you home at five on the dot each evening,' she grinned. 'Part of the trouble my client is having is because he often finds he works best at night and has been known to wake his secretary in the small hours to take masses of dictation!'

Beth shrugged, avoiding Allie's eyes, telling her, 'That won't be a problem. Charles has to spend a great deal of time away from home himself,' and that was the truth. Since the accident he'd been away more often than not. 'He won't mind at all if I'm away for a few weeks.' And that was true, too. He and Zanna would be very happy if she were to make herself scarce. They wouldn't want her to hang around, making scenes, once they'd explained what was going on. And she didn't want that either. She would beat a dignified retreat. It was, after all, the only thing she could do.

She stood up gracefully, her natural poise coming to her aid. Allie could make what she liked of the situation and one day she, Beth, would tell her friend the truth behind it all. But not yet. She wasn't strong enough to face the sympathy, the 'I told you so's. And she was more than thankful that her parents were away, taking the world cruise they'd promised themselves when her father had retired.

'Give me a ring tomorrow, would you?' she asked. 'After you've fixed everything.'

'I can do better than that,' Allie said, her brown eyes serious. 'If you can promise me that Charles Savage of South Park doesn't live up to his name and come to beat me up for sending his wife abroad.'

'That's about the last thing he'd do.' Beth made herself smile, aching inside because she knew the reverse was true. Charles would probably send Allie champagne and flowers for months for so opportunely helping him to rid himself of a wife he no longer wanted, the wife he had never pretended to love.

'If you say so!' But Allie was already reaching for the phone, punching numbers and, five minutes later, after intense conversation, she replaced the receiver and told Beth, 'He's weak with relief, or so he tells me. He has work piling up to the ceiling and you can't get there soon enough.' She scribbled rapidly on a card and handed it over to Beth. 'His address and phone number. If you get lost, you're to ring and he'll come to your rescue. And the same applies if you want meeting at Boulogne. Shall you fly, or cross by ferry?'

'Take the car on the ferry.' Beth tucked the pasteboard into her handbag and rose to go. If she was going to be completely independent then she might as well start now, and, although her heart was beating like a drum as she turned the Metro through South Park's gateposts, her soft mouth was set in lines of sheer determination, her green eyes cool.

Charles had made no secret of his reason for marrying her. He had wanted an heir, a family to enjoy all he had achieved. That he had distanced himself from her, emotionally and physically, after she had lost their child and the prognosis for her ever conceiving again had been unhopeful, had come as no surprise. What did surprise her, in retrospect, was her stupidity in agreeing to marry him in the first place. She had been besotted, she thought grimly, young enough and gullible enough to believe that she could teach him to love her.

But then, she excused as she garaged the car and locked it behind her, she hadn't known that Zanna would come back, bringing their love-child along with her. How could she have known? She would have run a mile if she had been able to look into the future because, although she had been prepared to fight for Charles Savage's love, she didn't stand the ghost of a chance when Zanna was around. She never had done, and never would, and her strength lay in recognising that miserable and unalterable fact of life.

Her head was high as she walked through the hall and up the stairs. The whole house felt empty, very silent. Maybe Harry was still having his afternoon sleep and Charles and Zanna were taking advantage of it. She tried to tell herself she didn't care, but knew she did. The pain was almost too much to bear.

But she had to hold on. Had to pretend she was leaving of her own free will. Entering her room, she began to pack methodically, forcing herself to stay calm because if she let go, only for an instant, she would fall to pieces. And when she was ready to leave she would find Charles, say her piece and go, and that would be that. But it didn't work out like that, things never did, because Charles walked in through her door, making her jump out of her skin, and she spun round on her heels, her hand to her throat, her face running with fire.

And he said tautly, his austerely attractive features hard, 'Do you have a few free moments to spare for Zanna and me, yet?'

Beth shuddered suddenly, her whole body going cold. Ignoring the initial sarcasm coming from him, she saw his smoky eyes narrow as they fell on the open suitcase, and she got in quickly, 'I don't particularly want to hear whatever it is you and Zanna feel you want to say. It can't be important.' She turned her back on him, not willing for him to read the misery on her face.

She had to walk away from him before he got the chance to throw her out of his life; it was the only way she could salvage her pride, regain her self-respect. She wouldn't let herself crawl, or weep. Not in front of him, especially not when his old and only love was somewhere near—with the son the two of them had created together.

She heard the sudden angry hiss of indrawn breath a mere milli-second before his hard hands clamped down on her shoulders, dragging her round to face him, and her chin tilted up rebelliously as he grated blackly, 'What the hell's got into you?'

She could have told him, but wouldn't give him the satisfaction, or the opportunity to put his love, his need for Zanna and his son, into words. She could bear anything but that.

'Please let me go.' The heat from those strong fingers seared her skin through the thin fabric of her blouse, threatening to rob her of all her hard-won poise, and when his grip merely tightened she ground out quickly, hoping his anger at her refusal to listen to what he and his precious Zanna had to tell her would prevent him from guessing just how much his touch affected her, 'If you'll stop mauling me, I'll say what's on my mind.'

At the acid inflexion of her tone his hands dropped to his sides, his mouth going hard. It had worked like a charm, and if he thought his very touch disgusted her then that was a bonus. And she said tightly, before her will-power deserted her completely, 'I don't need to tell you how our marriage has been disintegrating these past few months.' She didn't specify dates, although she could have done, to the day. She couldn't bear to remind him, or herself, of the tragedy that had marked his loss of interest in her. 'I think it's best if we have a trial separation.'

She turned from him then, forcing herself to make her movements smooth and sure, taking a pile of lingerie from her dresser and adding it to the contents of her suitcase. Her heart was beating with a heavy, sickly rhythm, but he couldn't know that, and, although she couldn't see him, she was fully aware of the tense watchful look in those narrowed gunfighter's eyes, the tension that would be holding that powerfully crafted body rigid.

'Is that what you want?' There was a tightness in that deep husky voice that, had she not known better, she could have imagined to be pain. But she did know better, she reminded herself scornfully. He might not love her, and he assuredly wasn't planning on being faithful, but he wasn't an uncaring man and might be concerned about her future welfare.

Beth nodded, unable to speak for the moment because this was goodbye, wasn't it? Goodbye to the man she had always loved, to the future they might have had together had things worked out differently. Swallowing the painful lump in her throat, she bent to snap her case shut, the wings of her short, sleekly styled hair falling forwards to hide her face as she struggled to find her voice.

And then she managed, 'It is. I've got a job to go to, so you have no need to worry, and I suggest we get in touch in a month or two, to finalise things.' By then the whole locale would know she had gone, that Zanna had replaced her, returned to where she belonged. And by that time, although she knew she would never get over the pain, she would have created her own life away from him, gained in self-respect. And something bitter, deep inside her, made her add, 'And don't slam the door as you leave. It might wake Harry.'

'We might as well call it a day.' William Templeton dragged his fingers through his wiry light-brown hair, his craggy face drawn with fatigue. 'And thank you, Beth. We've done some good work—I can feel it in my bones.' His radiant smile suddenly flashed, transforming his plain, craggy features and Beth smiled back, she couldn't help herself; he was that kind of man.

She could even forgive him for knocking her up at four this morning, his fertile mind bursting with ideas for the mid section of his current book which had proved, up until then, a sticking point.

'Coffee?' Beth closed her shorthand notebook and laid it down beside the ancient electric typewriter on the cluttered desk, but William shook his head.

'I'm going to crash out for a couple of hours, and I suggest you do the same. If you're still asleep at noon I'll make lunch and wake you. OK?'

She nodded absently as he bumbled out of the book-filled study, physical tiredness and the relief of achievement making him look older than his forty years, making his chunky body in the worn old cords and battered sweater sag. And, momentarily, her green eyes softened.

During the ten days she'd been at the old farmhouse she had grown to like and respect the author. Despite his enormous commercial success he gave no signs of self-importance and although he worked her hard he was fair, paying excellent wages, insisting that she took plenty of time off to make up for his erratic working methods.

But although she had worked at full stretch for the last five hours, taking down his rapid-fire dictation, she was in no mood to go back to bed. She wouldn't sleep, she would simply lie there, prey to the thoughts she was still struggling to keep at bay.

Ten days wasn't nearly enough time to recover from the trauma of losing Charles, she told herself as she took herself off upstairs to shower in the slope-ceilinged bathroom beneath the eaves. She doubted if she would ever recover but hoped that,

with time, she would come to terms with it, would
be able to get on with her life without having to
guard her thoughts and emotions so completely.

Coming to France had been the best thing she
could have done, she assured herself as, dressed now
in a full emerald-green cotton skirt and a navy
sleeveless top, she made and drank some coffee in
the heavily beamed farmhouse kitchen.

William, bless him, kept her hard at work, leaving
her little time to fret. On her arrival he had greeted
her as if she were a saviour and her self-esteem had
been further enhanced when he'd praised her lavishly for the way she had tackled the piles of dog-
eared hand-written manuscript that had accumu-
lated since he had been without a secretary.

But Mariette Voisin, who came in most days to
tackle the housework, would be arriving at any
moment and, although the elderly French woman
spoke only garbled English, she was incorrigibly
curious and subjected Beth to a barrage of almost
unintelligible questions at every opportunity, so she
rinsed out the earthenware coffee-cup she had been
using and slipped out into the morning sunshine.

The converted farmhouse lay in a leafy hollow
along a tangle of narrow lanes between Boulogne
and Le Wast and when Beth had eventually
managed to find it, that first day, she had known
it would be the perfect place to hide.

Hide from whom? she scorned, kicking out at
one of the pebbles that littered the dusty lane. No
need to hide when no one would come looking.
Charles would be only too thankful that she had
voluntarily removed herself from his life.

Frowning, she pushed the intrusive thoughts of him out of her mind, deliberately trying to relax. Crouched over her shorthand notebook for five long hours made her body crave air and exercise and here, in these lovely sun-drenched lanes with the thick forest trees never far away, was the perfect place to take it. And suddenly, as often seemed to happen in this enchanted land, she rounded a bend and came across a hidden hump-backed stone bridge which spanned a dancing stream, and leant there, catching her breath, grateful for the shade of the overhanging trees.

Then, as the sound of an engine disarranged the sleepy pattern of birdsong and bees, she flattened herself against the parapet, leaving as much passing space as possible on the narrow track, then turned as the vehicle stopped behind her, probably a tourist, bemused by the seemingly aimless wandering of the lanes.

But the polite half-smile died on her soft lips and her heart flipped, stopped, then raced on. And Charles said from the open car window, 'Get in.'

She couldn't move. She literally couldn't move a muscle. She didn't know what he was doing here, how he had found her, why he had bothered. She opened her mouth, but no words came, and she just knew she must look like a dying fish, and that made hot colour run from the slash of her V neckline to the roots of her hair; then she heard him mutter a violent expletive as he slid out of the car to tower over her.

'Don't give me that blank stare, woman. We have met before.' His teeth closed with a snap, his eyes raking her pale face. 'I'm the man you married,

remember? Promising to love, honour and obey.
So get in the car.'

His strong hands were clenched at his sides,
bunched against the black denim of his jeans. He
looked as if he would like to shake her until her
head dropped off, and she pushed the word 'no'
past her dry lips and saw his mouth go tight, the
skin growing taut across the hard cheekbones and
aggressive jaw.

'I'm blocking the road and I'm not moving
another inch without you.' And that should have
given her fair warning of his intention to man-
handle her into the passenger-seat, but she was still
in shock while he walked round the front.

When he slid in beside her she managed huskily,
'I'm here on a job and I'm already late back,' which
was a downright lie but one he seemed to swallow
because he said, his deep voice silky smooth now
with an underlying menace she had never heard
from him before,

'So direct me. I'll take you there.'

And there was no way she was going to be able
to get out of that. She could refuse point-blank and
he would simply drive away with her. Anywhere,
the mood he was in. She had never seen him this
angry before.

Something inside her shivered and contracted as
she glanced up at his stony profile, and she gave
directions in a thin, sharp voice and wondered if
he knew just what kind of hell he was putting her
through.

She had just set her foot on the long, tough road
back to some sort of acceptance of her ruined marriage and he had to appear to plunge her back to

square one. And she was shaking inside as she said into the prickly silence, 'How did you know where I was?'

'Allie, who else?'

Of course. Who else? Beth and her best friend from schooldays had kept in close touch even after she'd married and left the Helpline Agency. She would have been the first person Charles would have asked.

'But why bother?' she asked dully, slowly, unconsciously, shaking her head.

He shot her a hard sideways look, a look that boded ill for her peace of mind, and his voice was grim as he told her, 'Did you think for one moment I'd simply let you walk away?'

CHAPTER THREE

BETH sagged in her seat, her eyes closing. Now why hadn't she thought of that? Of course he wouldn't allow her to simply walk away, to take that sort of initiative.

Charles Savage's middle name had to be determination. A tough character, he always had to be in control. He hated loose ends. He would have to know exactly what his estranged wife was doing, and where she was doing it. Besides, he would want a quick divorce, wouldn't he? He would need to keep tabs on her, know exactly where she was.

'Very cosy.' The biting edge of sarcasm as he braked the car made her eyes wing open. They were in the cobbled yard at the front of the old stone farmhouse, the tubs of geraniums around the walls making bright splashes of colour.

'Yes, isn't it?' She was giving as good as she got. He might have brought her down, but she wasn't out for the count—not as far as he was going to be allowed to see. 'I love it. I'm quite at home here already.'

Home. The very word cut through her like a blade. Home was where he was, and she would never be there again. Never was such a desolate word but she resolutely blinked back tears and shot him a bright, glittering look, ignoring the curl of anger on his mouth.

'Come along in, if you have something to say. You can't have come all this way just for a change of scenery.'

She let herself out of the car and swept over the yard ahead of him, willing herself to stay calm. So far she had avoided the agony of hearing him tell her he wanted a divorce, wanted to be free to marry Zanna and take her and their son to live with him.

She had run, but not far enough or fast enough, and he had caught up with her like Nemesis. And she was going to have to listen now, and not betray a thing.

If he knew how long she had loved him, how passionately, he would feel sorry for her. And that she could not, would not stand. The humiliation would be the final, deadly straw. Far better, for both of them, if he continued to believe that theirs had been a loveless marriage, on both sides, and that she had decided that that type of sterile relationship was no longer enough.

It was silent in the square, stone-flagged hall and he stood in the open doorway behind her, blocking out the sun, and his voice was ice as he remarked, 'Just the two of you, is it? You and the celebrated author? Quite an idyllic set-up.'

'As you say.' Her voice was brittle, hard. It had to be, because to deny what he was obviously thinking would be to reveal a tiny chink in her armour. No need to tell him that she slept in the annexe, as had her predecessor, had her own small private sitting-room with a tiny bathroom above, built into the roof, and only came into the main house to work, to take her meals. No need to let him know that, loving him, no other man really existed for her.

'Come through to the sitting-room,' she invited, her level tone belying the sickening race of her heartbeats. 'William's still in bed, but I'm sure he won't mind, in the circumstances.'

She went to move away, towards the door next to the study, but her wrist was caught in a grip of steel and his mouth was a bitter line as he snapped, hauling her against the hard, lean length of his body, 'Had a hard night, did he?'

'We both did!' Being so close, feeling his vital body warmth, the hard thrust of perfectly honed muscle and bone beneath the casual jeans and sweatshirt, was bitter-sweet torment and her taunt was in direct response, a defence mechanism she had no control over, and she put defiance into her eyes, to hide the anguish, meeting his, seeing the involuntary jerk of a muscle at the side of his jaw, feeling a tiny stab of triumph because he, after all, could be jealous.

But the triumph was hollow, short-lived. She was still his wife and, as such, his property. He had wedded and bedded her, and her body, for three short months, had carried his child. And then he had never made love to her again because, knowing the odds on her ever conceiving again were impossibly long, there had been no point. Yet, even so, he still regarded her as his possession; his masculine ego would snarl at the the thought of her going to bed with any other man.

Her throat clogged with misery, she tried to drag herself away, but his grip merely tightened and his voice was thick as he stated, 'Beth, we have to talk.

Don't you see that?' And for an insane moment she almost believed he cared, that there was still something left of their marriage, that something could be salvaged from the ruins. Slowly, she looked up at him from between her long dark lashes, felt a betraying tremor run through his body, and heard William say from the head of the stairs,

'Is everything all right, Beth?' His voice was roughly aggressive because it wasn't every day he came across a total stranger manhandling his secretary.

So the moment was over, and she must have imagined that jealousy, and had to put it down to wishful thinking because Charles, when he answered for her, sounded almost bored, completely urbane, totally in control.

'Perfectly all right, Templeton. I was passing and decided to drop in on my wife.'

'Oh. I see.' He sounded wary, coming down the stairs slowly, and Beth sighed.

When she had first arrived she had told her employer that she was separated from her husband. A broken marriage was nothing unusual these days. And he had accepted that, and if he had jumped to the conclusion that the separation was of long duration, and amicable, she hadn't put him right.

She had been feeling too raw to go into any details. And now he probably imagined that he would come down each morning to find an irate husband on his doorstep.

That kind of complication she could do without! And if she wanted to keep her job she would have to convince him otherwise.

'Beth, would you ask Mariette to bring coffee to the study—you'll join us, Savage?' William faced the younger, much taller man, his expression faintly belligerent. He had obviously showered recently and changed into lightweight fawn trousers and a crisp white shirt, looking far more alert after his sleep, younger, tougher.

'Thank you.' Charles dipped his dark head, the tone of his voice almost contemptuous, his mouth grim, and Beth slipped away, the palms of her hands slicked with perspiration.

The two men were acting like adversaries, circling each other, ready to fight to the death for their territorial rights. She couldn't understand it. She might still be married to Charles but that state of affairs wouldn't last long because he wanted to be rid of her. And although William might be annoyed because his working routine was being disrupted by an unwelcome visitor, he must know that it was a one-off, wouldn't happen again.

She would have to make that very clear as soon as Charles left. She needed this job and had every intention of keeping it, intending, once she had proved herself capable and reliable, to ask if he would employ her on a permanent footing.

Mariette wasn't in the kitchen so Beth made the coffee herself, glad of the respite. Seeing Charles again, so soon, had been a shock and she needed time to brace herself to act as if she didn't really care when he asked her for a divorce.

But she couldn't make the simple task last all morning and when she carried the tray into the study she was no nearer gaining total control over her emotions than she had been when Charles had appeared out of the blue, bundling her into his car.

And the atmosphere inside the small, book-lined room did nothing to help her equilibrium. William was behind his desk, his eyes glowering, and Charles was pacing the floor, like a caged tiger trying to break out.

'How long are you staying in the area?' William questioned abruptly.

Charles, his narrowed eyes watching every move Beth made as she poured coffee, answered silkily, 'As long as I need to,' his steely grey eyes hardening as she handed him his cup. 'Making yourself indispensable to yet another man?'

Although fiery colour washed her face Beth's body went icy cold. That had been a direct reference to the fact that, for six months before he had come out with his astonishing proposal of marriage, she had worked as a temporary housekeeper-cum-social-hostess at South Park.

Beth remembered, as if it were yesterday, the morning when Charles had walked into the Helpline Agency. Mrs Penny, he'd explained, had fallen and broken her hip and it would be months before she would be fit for work again. And everyone knew that, not long before, Zanna had walked out of his life, leaving him bereft. Her heart had ached for him, because she had known what it was like to love hopelessly. But at least Charles had known a spell of intense happiness with the woman everyone knew he was obsessed by.

'I need a miracle—a Jill of all trades,' he'd confessed, his austere features softening in a smile which looked rarely used these days. 'Someone to act as temporary housekeeper, occasional secretary and sometime hostess when I entertain business colleagues for working weekends. It would be for some months, certainly until Mrs Penny is fit to return. But by then I should have got something sorted out regarding the other duties.'

To this day, Beth didn't know just what madness had prompted her to offer. Heaven knew, she and Allie had been busy enough with administering the rapidly expanding agency, and her secret love for Charles Savage, that hopeless thing that had refused to die the death or go away, would merely be fanned into a raging conflagration if she were foolish enough to spend so much time with him.

But Charles had had no such qualms, of course. Why on earth should he? He'd been openly relieved, and even the brooding severity of those gunfighter's eyes—and everyone around had noticed just how much more brooding they had become since Zanna Hall had left him—had lightened to silvery pleasure as he'd told her,

'That would be ideal. Living in the village, you'd be able to go home each evening, and as I shall be working in the City for most of the week you'll have plenty of time to organise the weekend arrangements when I decide to entertain. And there is daily help with the cleaning and so on, so you won't find stepping into Mrs Penny's shoes as well too arduous.'

But, as it had happened, he had spent far less time away than he had led her to expect, and her stupid, hopeless love for him had been fanned, just as she had privately predicted . . .

And William was perceptive enough to pick up her distress now because when she judged her hand was steady enough to carry his coffee to him his kindly eyes looked directly into hers with compassion—and just the hint of a question. Then he turned to Charles, whose silence seemed to contain a threat.

'Where are you staying?'

'In Boulogne.' He named one of the most prestigious hotels, his voice curt, and put his half-finished coffee down on the tray. 'But I haven't come here to exchange pleasantries. I'd like a word with Beth. In private.' He stalked to the door, as if he could no longer endure the confinement. And he cut through the beginning of the older man's expostulations with a grim, 'I realise she's your secretary, Templeton, but first and foremost she is my wife.'

In the tense, waiting silence, Beth heard the drumbeat of her own blood as she resisted the urge to scream. She felt like a bone being tugged between two snarling dogs, and didn't know why.

'Beth?' William's voice sounded indecisive. 'Is that what you want?'

She nodded mutely. Charles, in this mood, would get exactly what he wanted and wouldn't care about the methods he used. And as he was here they might as well get the unhappy discussion about their future out of the way. And when that was settled she could make her peace with her employer, reassure him that he wasn't about to be caught up in the middle of a nasty ongoing matrimonial drama. Once Charles had her agreement to a rapid divorce, he most certainly wouldn't want to set eyes on her

again, much less waste his precious time in seeking
her out and causing disruption at her place of work.

Charles was standing at the door, waiting, the
dark line of his brow impatient, and Beth walked
reluctantly towards him, her stomach lurching, her
feet like lead. Hearing him put his request for a
divorce into words was going to be one of the worst
things that had ever happened to her.

But she would survive it, she told herself firmly
as, her head held high, she walked through the door,
refusing to meet his eyes.

'Here!'

She had walked out into the sun-drenched
morning, making for the stone bench against one
of the courtyard walls, instinctively knowing that
she would need to be sitting down while she listened to what he had to say to her. Already her legs
were shaking. But she turned at his barked
command, saw he was holding the car door open
for her, and sucked in a ragged breath.

'Don't treat me like a dog!' she snapped, forcing
anger through her bloodstream. Better anger than
helpless misery, far better. 'I don't come to heel at
your command.'

'So I'm beginning to notice. Nevertheless, get in.'

'Whatever you have to say to me can be said
here.' She stood her ground, digging her heels in.
'There's no one around, it's quite private.'

'I have no intention of staying on Templeton's
property,' he told her grimly. 'So do you come will-
ingly, or do I have to make you?'

Beth compressed her lips to trap a shuddering
sigh. The warning in his ruthless gaze was unmistakable. Better to get into the car under her own

steam than have him put her there. If he touched
her again her body would betray her, demonstrate
how much she still wanted, needed and loved him.
And she couldn't think why he had taken such an
instant dislike to the harmless William. He should
be shaking the other man's hand, slapping him on
the back because he had, after all, provided his unwanted wife with a job, a wage and living
accommodation!

She shuddered violently as he slammed the car
door behind her as soon as she'd settled in the passenger-seat, biting down on her lower lip as he
stalked round to take his place. She had known he
was capable of anger; she'd had enough confi-
dential conversations with the wives of his em-
ployees and business colleagues who'd accompanied
their husbands on those working weekends at South
Park to learn that though he was always fair-
minded, willing to listen to the other person's point
of view, his icy anger when someone failed to live
up to his exacting standards was something to be
avoided at all costs.

But she, herself, had never experienced it until
now. It made her feel small and vulnerable, threatened, as if she didn't know him at all, as if he had
become a dangerous, menacing stranger.

While they were leaving the courtyard and
heading for open country at what Beth considered
to be a dangerous speed, she forced herself to stare
grimly ahead, to display no emotion at all. She
wasn't even going to ask where the hell he thought
he was taking her. She couldn't trust her voice.

And he was silent, too, handling the fast car with
steely concentration. Beth wasn't surprised. Since

the accident the lines of communication between them had broken down.

Previously, they'd always been able to talk, about everything under the sun. And that was just one of the things that had further cemented her love for him when she had first gone to work for him at South Park.

Eventually, he braked the car at the foot of a forest track, the tyres spinning, scattering small stones, and Beth let herself out of the car, closing the door and leaning against it with weak relief.

The tension, the unspoken rage coming from him had been more than she could bear and she dragged in a deep breath of the slightly cooler air, scented by the forest trees, spiced by the faint tang of the ocean, and rubbed the beads of perspiration from her short upper lip with the back of a clenched hand.

And he was standing in front of her, a dark, silent presence whose soft-footed approach made her heart leap and twist inside her.

But there was something different now, as if the concentration needed to handle the fast car with safety had exorcised that coiling anger. And her unguarded eyes winged up to his, then dropped, veiled by heavy lids and the thick dark sweep of her lashes as she recognised the softening of his eyes, his features.

Compassion? Pity? She didn't need it. He had always treated her with kindliness and respect, even after she had lost the child he had set his heart on. He would be feeling sorry for her, knowing he was about to tell her exactly why Zanna had returned after all this time.

He wasn't a deliberately cruel man; he wouldn't want to cause her pain. But there was nothing he could do about it because Zanna, for him, had been an obsession. Still was. Always would be. Everyone had known that, which was why the people who really cared about her, her parents and Allie, had warned her against accepting his marriage proposal.

She should have listened to them. She'd been too sure of her ability to make him forget the other woman, learn to love her. She had been so sure he would, especially when she gave him the child he had told her he wanted.

'Come, we'll walk.' His deep voice was thick with what had to be regret for what he was about to do to her. But she didn't want his pity. She wanted his love but had never had it. And never would now.

'Come,' he repeated, and held out one hand. But she pointedly ignored it, stepping aside, giving him a wide berth as she began to walk up the lonely forest track. And he followed, overtaking her easily, anger back in every rapid stride as he thrust onwards, taking a narrower, rarely used track, and she tagged after him because there was nothing else to do and he would only drag her along, the mood he was in, if she gave in to her instincts and sat down on the loamy floor of the forest and put back her head and howled.

And just when she thought she was fated to follow him through this lonely place for all time he flung over his shoulder, 'When you walked out on me you should have said you couldn't bear to touch me. I just might not have bothered finding you!'

'I don't know why you did!' she hurled right back, her breath coming rapidly, due more to the knowledge that they were at last beginning the final confrontation than the pace he had set.

As long as he never discovered just how much she longed for his touch and how often, during the past three months, she had cried herself to sleep, aching for the physical intimacy they had once shared and which he, for obvious reasons, shunned, she would be able to hang on to the new beginnings of her self-respect.

'I would have thought you'd be far too busy back at South Park with Zanna—and young Harry!'

They had reached a clearing, the tall trees like a cathedral vault overhead, golden sunlight filtering through, making the silent shadows dimmer. And he stopped, and turned, facing her, and, for a moment, an image of pain flickered over his face. And then nothing. His features could have been carved from marble as he told her, 'I understand your jealousy. But don't let it warp your very existence. I promise you, Beth, there will be others for you.'

She didn't know how she stopped herself from slapping him, stopped herself from yelling out all her disgust and rage. But she managed it, remembering in time that, believing as he did that their marriage had been without love on both sides, he would naturally assume that she would find someone else.

And now was the time to get everything straight, and she steeled herself for that, wondering if he could hear the heavy, panicky beat of her heart in this dim green silence.

Taking a hold on herself, she told him calmly, 'I know why Zanna came back with Harry. I over-heard you talking together the day they arrived.'

There, it was out. He had no need now to break the 'news'. And she heard him drag in his breath and then expel it slowly, the tight span of his shoulders relaxing beneath the soft dark fabric of his sweatshirt.

'So at least you understand about that.' His fine eyes darkened with something she couldn't put a name to and, almost too late, she saw the trap she had walked into.

She had told him she'd overheard that conver-sation, and she knew he would be remembering, too, the things that had been said. How he'd already told the woman he loved that the ill-begotten mar-riage he'd entered into with the unsuitable Beth Garner was over. And how, because of that, Zanna had returned, bringing their son. She'd done her best as a single parent, but Harry needed his father, too.

Fleetingly, Beth wondered why Zanna had walked out on Charles in the first place. Their deep, ob-sessive love for each other had been the talk of the neighbourhood gossips for months.

Then, quickly, she pushed those thoughts out of her head, painfully aware of Charles's intent gaze. One way or another she had to extricate herself, step back from the trap she had almost walked straight into.

Somehow, Charles had to be made to believe a lie, believe that she had walked out on him, not because Zanna had returned and Charles wanted a divorce, but because she, Beth, had decided she'd had enough.

Walking out on him before he could ask her to go was the only way to salvage her pride. She had nothing else left.

'Of course I understand,' she told him crisply, resisting the impulse to hug her arms around her slender body because, despite the warmth of the day, she was cold inside, aching with it. 'But it isn't really important. It was nothing to do with my reasons for wanting a separation.'

'Which were?' He had moved closer to her and the very forest trees seemed to hold their breath. Beth couldn't speak, her heart beating crazily, making her head spin.

She couldn't lie to him, not about a thing like that, she agonised, looking up at him, the bones of his face tight with tension. She simply couldn't do it. How could she deny her love for him? The love that had been growing, maturing and strengthening since she was fifteen years old?

'Your reasons, Beth?' he pressed darkly, his eyes narrowing as they swept her anguished features.

She flung out breathlessly, retreating, 'The same as yours, I imagine. We both know what these last few months have been like. The marriage simply didn't work out.'

And he could translate that any way he wished, she thought distractedly, trying to stifle a betraying sob. And the most likely interpretation he would put on her evasive answer would be to believe that she, like himself, had grown tired of the sterile relationship, had long since reached the stage when even physical interest was totally dead. The way she had refused to take his hand back there, avoiding his touch, would reinforce that opinion.

'I don't believe this.' He looked as if she had slapped him, and she didn't understand—her brain was too confused and tired to work anything out. And why didn't he simply take what she had handed him on a plate, cut and run—right back home to the eagerly waiting Zanna? Why drag this awful confrontation out?

She couldn't stand much more of this. Her emotions had been dragging her down ever since she had eavesdropped on that conversation, trying to avoid the inevitable, running away when he'd told her that he and Zanna had something to say to her.

Weakly, she closed her eyes, doing nothing to prevent the hot salty tears that trickled down her cheeks. All she wanted was for him to leave her alone, allow her some dignity. He had got exactly what he wanted, hadn't he? Did he have to have his pound of flesh, too?

'Beth. Don't.' His voice was raw and before she knew what was happening his arms were around her, dragging her close into his body, and for one insane moment she allowed herself to melt, to cling to him, blocking her mind to the way things were.

'Tell me what's wrong,' he whispered darkly, one strong hand cradling her head into the solid angle of his shoulder, and the blood began to beat thickly through her veins, drugging her, and only when his other hand began a slow caressing movement along the length of her spine did she realise what she was doing.

She was allowing him to take the initiative, all over again, as he always had in their relationship.

Not content with tossing her aside as soon as the woman he really loved appeared back on the scene, he wanted a run-down on her battered feelings.

Well, she wasn't going to pander to his male ego. Wrenching her head away from its dangerous resting place, she bunched her hands into small fists and pushed against his shoulders, at the end of her tether, grinding out, 'Leave me alone, can't you?'

Her efforts to push him away were worse than futile; they seemed to be heightening his desire to subdue her, she thought frantically, noting the rapid rise and fall of his deep chest, the savage glitter of his narrowed eyes as he tightened his hold on her squirming body and bit out, 'Why the hell should I? You're still my wife, damn it!'

And then the world went very still, very silent, only the chaotic drumbeats of her heart sounding wildly in her ears, only her own sobbing, burning breath, the quick, rasping hiss that escaped his clamped lips before his mouth possessed hers in a brutal kiss that was like nothing that had ever gone before, his big body subduing her panicky attempts to escape, carrying them both down to the soft forest floor, down and down to a hot dark warmth from which there was no way out. A burning, feverish heat, all sense and reason gone because, although he no longer wanted her in his life, she was still, legally, his possession, and he was stamping his brand, this one last time, just to prove his domination.

And this was going to be rape.

CHAPTER FOUR

BUT it wasn't rape. Of course it wasn't.

As far as Charles was concerned, Beth's responsive body was all fire and fury, matching his own. It had been so long since he had touched her, wanted her, that when she felt his hard body covering hers all logical thought flew out of her head, her arms reaching up to twine around him, gathering him closer.

And, as if her eager response triggered a more caring approach, the tenderness that had always been an intrinsic part of his passion in the early days of their marriage, his kiss gentled, his mouth tasting hers now, exploring a world within a world, searching, finding the gateway to her soul.

Because her soul, her heart, her mind and body would always belong to him, no matter what happened, Beth thought, and closed her mind off as his sure fingers undid the buttons of her top and slid the soft fabric from her gleaming satiny shoulders, and surrendered herself to him and the moment—the future, the past no longer important.

Groaning softly, he buried his face in her breasts and her throat arched back, her hands avidly stroking the magnificent breadth of his back beneath his sweatshirt, the strong arch of his ribcage.

It wasn't a journey of discovery; she was simply coming home. She knew and worshipped every inch of his hard male body, and when he lifted his head and looked at her from narrowed, glittering eyes, she could only whisper his name.

'Kiss me,' he commanded roughly, his skin pulled tight across his angular cheekbones, and she lifted eager hands to his head, her fingers twisting in the dark softness of his hair as she pulled him down, her lush lips parted, receptive.

And when she thought she would die from the sweet, melting torment of his mouth he rolled away from her, his eyes holding hers with scorching intensity as his hands went to the buckle of the leather belt that spanned his narrow waist. And her whole body was shaken with fine tremors of need.

For far, far too long she had ached for the love he had denied her and their mating on the soft forest floor was explosive, a wild, tumultuous release that left her satiated, her delicate body bruised by passion, curling immediately into the sheltering warmth of his as she fell asleep with the utter suddenness of a child.

Waking slowly, Beth felt flutters of cool air beating against her naked skin and she made a tiny mewing sound of distress then opened her eyes, focusing on the tall, dusk-shadowed man. He was fully dressed now, zipping up his jeans, and, at her small sound of protest, he was on his knees in front of her, his hands rubbing her arms and shoulders, his voice rough at the edges as he told her,

'You're cold. I'll help you dress.'

And he did, his fingers deft and sure, making up for her clumsiness. Her brain was in shock at what had happened, the lovemaking he had forced upon her to begin with but which she, craven idiot that she was, had then actively encouraged.

She felt so ashamed of herself that she wanted to die.

She had slept in his arms for hours, his body half covering her, keeping her warm, and now she was stiff and cold, back to reality, the fantasy and magic all gone.

Because there had been no magic at all, she reminded herself as she forced her feet into her sandals, merely stupidity on her part and the natural masculine desire to brand a possession—even if he no longer actually wanted it.

Ineffectively trying to smooth the crumpled folds of her skirt, she whimpered her self-disgust, and Charles said thickly, his face remote, 'Have my sweatshirt.' He was already beginning to strip it off and although the extra warmth would have been welcome it would be his warmth. She shook her head impatiently.

'No, thanks,' she said, and set off quickly down the track. 'I have to get back.' Back to the security of the old farmhouse, her own little room. She would think about how to explain her long absence to William some other time. Just now the degrading way she had behaved left no room for anything else in her head.

One minute she'd been telling her husband that she understood why he'd taken his former mistress back into his life, saying that, in any case, she had been thinking about a separation for some time, implying that he could have the divorce he so obviously wanted if he were to legitimise his son. And the next... Well, the next minute she had been locked in his arms, writhing around on the forest floor, practically begging him to make love to her!

'Beth.' He caught her arm, just above her elbow, swinging her round to face him. It was already late afternoon and the heavy canopy of leaves cut out the light and his face was shadowed, remote. 'We have to talk.'

'Not now!' She dragged her arm away and watched his hands fall to his sides, his mouth clamping in a grim line. She swung away again, her slender shoulders rigid with temper.

How could he expect her to discuss the divorce he wanted, sordid things like settlements or whatever, when he had so recently filled her body with the explosion of his passion? How could he bring that hateful subject up? Couldn't he see how she was almost disintegrating with self-disgust, her anger the only thing keeping her together?

And she snapped through her teeth, 'Just drive me home. I never want to see you again!'

'If that's what you want,' he ground out tightly, overtaking her with long, furious strides, stalking ahead and flinging over his shoulder, 'But Templeton's house is not your home. Never forget it!'

Dog in the manger, Beth thought angrily, her burning eyes boring into his back as he swung through the trees on the track ahead. He no longer wanted her as his wife, yet he couldn't bear the thought of her being with another man.

Not that her relationship with William was in any way sexual. She was here to do a job, and after taking off for the best part of the day, when what she and Charles had had to say to each other would have only needed ten minutes at most, she might not have a job to go back to, she thought sniffily.

Charles reached the car well ahead of her and was waiting, holding the door open, and she got in, not able to look at him because he had reduced her to the status of a plaything, had decided to indulge in one last sexual romp before he tossed her out of his life forever.

And she, poor fool, had urged him on! She disgusted herself, she really did!

He drove back to the farmhouse in silence—the air in the cabin of the car was thick with it—and as she fumbled to release her seatbelt he glanced at his watch, his brows drawn together in a heavy bar of impatience.

'Nothing's been resolved. Not a damn thing.' His fingers beat an irritated tattoo on the wheel and she slid out of the car quickly as he threatened, 'But I'll be back. Make no mistake about that.'

Her fingers quivering on the door, Beth retorted sharply, 'Don't bother. Make all the arrangements for the divorce through my solicitor,' and banged it shut, wincing as a moment later she heard the powerful engine roar to life, scattering the handful of foraging hens when the car shot out of the courtyard on an angry, full-throated snarl.

She was shivering with reaction as she crept round the side of the house, making for the kitchen. She couldn't face her employer until she'd pulled herself together. Trying to come up with a reason to excuse her hours-long absence wasn't going to be easy. She certainly couldn't tell him the truth, tell him that she'd spent the afternoon making love with her estranged husband, sleeping naked in his arms!

Mariette was in the kitchen, podding broad beans ready for the evening meal, her small black eyes gleaming with curiosity, and Beth could almost see the wheels in her brain turning as she tried to find the English words for the endless questions that were obviously right there on the end of her tongue.

Giving the housekeeper a wan smile, Beth scurried through to the annexe to the privacy and safety of her own room. It would be a long time before she got over the trauma of what had happened this afternoon, the disgust she felt for her own behaviour. She simply wasn't up to facing anyone until she could face herself.

But she would have to face William, she reminded herself sharply as she emerged from the shower and dressed in a fresh skirt and cotton-knit sweater. When his secretary disappeared for hours on end he was entitled to an explanation.

She found him in the airy sitting-room of the main house, the room they took their meals in, and he had his back to her, standing by the window with the pages of manuscript she'd typed previously in his hands. And he turned sharply as she entered and, amazingly, there was nothing on his bluntly good-looking face but relief.

'Are you all right? When you didn't come back I thought that brute had done something to you. I was beginning to panic.'

'I'm sorry.' Thick hot colour slid over Beth's face as vivid pictures of exactly what 'that brute' had done to her flooded her mind. But she couldn't put that into words, could she? And she began to gabble, 'Our—our discussion took longer than I'd bargained for. I'll make up the time, of course.'

'Don't even think of it,' William dismissed gruffly. 'Just as long as you're all right.' He moved

over to the table Mariette had already set, poured
wine and handed her a glass. 'Sit down and drink
this. You look as if you need it.' And as she gratefully sank down on to the sofa he sat beside her,
his big-knuckled hands hanging between his knees,
questioning, 'Was it to do with a divorce? When
you came here you told me you were separated. My
advice is, give him what he wants. He'll take it,
anyway—he looks that type.'

Beth nodded, too choked to speak, twisting the
stem of the wine glass around in her fingers, and
William patted her shoulder awkwardly, his voice
gruff as he added, 'There aren't any children, are
there?' and she shook her head.

No, there were no children. Just Harry. Just
Charles's son. But not hers, of course. Never hers.
She had lost her child, along with all her foolish
dreams of happiness, three long months ago.

Her eyes filled with sudden unstoppable tears and
William said quickly, 'I'm sorry. None of my
business. But if the brute's made you unhappy my
advice is cut and run. Forget him and don't look
back. It never pays. And don't forget, if you ever
want to talk it out, need a shoulder to lean on, I'm
here.' He had gone very pink, changing the subject
rapidly. 'I'm going to be up to my eyeballs in research tomorrow, so why don't you take the
morning off, go into Boulogne, have lunch and
bring back some fish for supper?'

'Are you sure you won't need me?' He was doing
his best to be kind, manufacturing an errand as an
excuse for her outing, despite the hours she'd wasted
today.

He was a dear, and not to know that she would much prefer to work flat out. Hard work was the only thing that would take her mind off her misery. But she couldn't throw his kindness back in his face, especially when he beamed, 'I've told you. I've got to get a few facts straight before I can go any further, and I prefer to do my own research. And I'm partial to fish, straight from the boats. See if you can get a couple of good sole.'

'Yes, of course.'

She did her best to look pleased, more than grateful that he hadn't bawled her out for disappearing for hours, staying away with the stranger who had invaded the privacy of his home, a stranger he obviously disliked as intensely as Charles disliked him. And, just for one weak moment, she was tempted to confide in her kindly employer.

It would be a relief to talk about the pain and misery she'd endured, the insecurity of knowing that her husband no longer pretended to want her in any meaningful way, the dreadful shock she'd sustained when Zanna had come back on the scene. She'd never talked about it to anyone, never hinted—even to her parents—that anything was wrong.

Sighing, she pushed the weak moment aside. Who was she to burden others with her misery? William was only her employer, after all. If she told him the whole truth she might only manage to embarrass him. No one wanted to be burdened with another's troubles. And she had their future working relationship to think of.

* * *

Beth parked her car on the quai Gambetta and made for the fish stalls, the pale lemon skirts of her light cotton dress swinging around her long, slender legs, the wind from the sea tossing her glossy dark hair, setting it flying around her face.

There was a spring in her step this morning, a half-excited, half-fearful hope in her heart, a hope she had tried to kill—and, having failed, was determined to act on.

She bought the fish William wanted, two large sole fresh from the boats, and hurried back to the car, oblivious to the bustle of locals and the British tourists who were buying the famous Boulogne mussels and oysters to take home on the ferry. At any other time she would have lingered, enjoying the sounds, sights and smells, used the holiday William had given her to explore the ancient town which Henry VIII of England had once captured and where Napoleon had spent three years preparing to invade in his turn.

But, even though she half feared she was going on a fool's errand, she had to see Charles. In answer to William's question he had given the name of his hotel and, before she steeled herself to face the irretrievable breakdown of her marriage to the only man she had ever loved, ever could love, she had to see him one last time.

Trying to steady her racing heartbeats, to warn herself that nothing might come of this one last meeting, she found a space on a multi-storey car park, rummaged in her handbag for her small hand-mirror and checked her reflection. Her huge green eyes were over-bright, feverish, too big for her small, pointed face. And her full, wide mouth still looked swollen from the passionate imprint of Charles's sensual onslaught. And there were lines of strain, too, deepening the hollows beneath her cheekbones, painting dark smudges beneath her eyes.

Pushing the mirror back into her bag, she snapped it shut decisively and left the car. Bewailing the havoc that was the result of a sleepless night wasn't going to achieve a thing.

She had lain awake, tormented by memories. For months, ever since the accident, he hadn't come near her, hadn't so much as touched her hand, carefully avoiding any physical contact, spending more and more time away from home.

Yet yesterday afternoon he had acted as if he was starving for her; his hoarse cry of male exultation as he had driven her to the wild heights of ecstatic fulfilment and then exploded cataclysmically inside the throbbing sheath of her body had surely been more than the climax of pleasure gained from having a final sexual fling with a wife he no longer cared about.

Could he have made love to her with such tumultuous passion, shown such tenderness, if she no longer meant anything to him? It was a question she couldn't answer, but was determined to ask.

If there was any hope, no matter how slight, for their marriage, then she was going to put up a fight to keep him, she vowed staunchly as she walked back down the hill from the old town, through the maze of little streets with their tempting shops and restaurants.

Praying he hadn't already left for home—last evening he'd clearly been pushed for time, as she'd noted when witnessing his impatient glance at his watch—she hurried on, her high heels tapping on the cobbles. If there was the remotest chance of saving their marriage then, clearly, he must recognise Harry as his son, see him regularly, make provision for his future.

Despite the loss of her own child, Beth was sure she could come to terms with such a state of affairs—if only she could be sure that his obsession with the boy's mother was a thing of the past!

'Well, well—look who's here!' The husky drawl was unmistakable and Beth's feet froze to the spot while cold apprehension crawled all over her body. She didn't believe this was happening, she simply didn't believe it!

She turned her head slowly towards the pavement tables outside the restaurant she'd been so blithely passing and her heart wrenched painfully inside her as she met Zanna's scornfully derisive eyes.

Her mouth dry as dust, she could only stand and stare, transfixed, as Zanna's lush scarlet lips parted in a parody of a smile.

'Charles said you were taking a working holiday—a euphemism, if ever I heard one.' She put her coffee-cup back on its saucer and leaned back in her chair, her red-gold hair curling on to the delicately tanned shoulders the low-cut white sundress she was wearing left bare. And her voice was brittle now. 'But we all know why you took to your heels, don't we? Your prim little mind couldn't face the fact of Harry's existence—you couldn't even bear to discuss the ramifications, could you? Not that your pigheaded cowardice makes a scrap of difference; what's happened has happened and even if your delicate sensibilities are offended you can't alter a thing.'

'I have no intention of trying.' Beth had found her voice now but it emerged sounding rusty, as if she hadn't used it in a long, long time.

Charles had sought her out for one purpose only—to discuss the divorce. And even then he hadn't been able to be parted from the woman he had loved for years, the woman who had only recently come back into his life. She wondered hysterically what the other woman would say if she told her how those discussions had never taken place and exactly how they'd been side-tracked!

But she held her tongue, biting back the bitter words because, although they would show Charles in a bad light, they would also reveal her own total vulnerability to him—the way she had behaved like a sex-starved wanton while he, as she had originally and logically believed, had only been putting his mark of possession on her for one last time—his sexual arousal down to the fact that he had disapproved of his titular wife living under the same roof as her employer.

And at that moment she hated everyone— Charles, Zanna, but most of all herself—and she clipped out emotionally, 'You can have what you want. It won't be long until your bastard can legitimately take the name of Savage!'

The moment the scathing words were out, she could have bitten her tongue off. None of this mess was the child's fault, and from what she had seen of him during that dreadful weekend he was utterly charming, a well adjusted, confident little boy who resembled Charles so strongly that every time she had looked at him her heart had contracted, breaking up a little more.

'I'm sorry,' she murmured huskily, appalled at herself, but Zanna obviously took no offence, the thickness of her skin unbelievable as she shrugged.

'You're quite right, of course. That's what I plan and that's what is going to happen.' And then, amazingly, she patted the vacant seat beside her. 'Sit down. Charles shouldn't be long. He took Harry to watch the ferry docking and we arranged to meet here.' She inspected the face of her tiny jewelled watch. 'He should be here any moment; we're flying south this afternoon.'

South to the sun, to the exotic playgrounds of France, where the two of them could enjoy a romantic idyll, making up for the wasted years when they had been apart, their tiny son completing their bonding. She might have known that he wouldn't install his mistress and son at South Park until after the divorce, when he could take her there as his wife.

'No. Thanks,' Beth muttered, feeling ill. Did Zanna really expect her to sit and wait for the husband who so patently wanted her out of his life? Did she really expect the three of them to sit together, drinking coffee, making polite and meaningless conversation? That sort of thing might happen in the sophisticated circles Zanna moved in, but to Beth the whole idea was incredible.

'As you like.' The other woman gave a careless shrug. 'Run and hide from the facts again—it doesn't bother me. I always knew you weren't woman enough to hold him.' She gave a vicious little smile. 'Charles is strong meat. I never did think you could cope with a man that sexually dangerous, that overpowering.'

Wordlessly, Beth stumbled away, tears of humiliation blinding her. Like every young girl around, just emerging into womanhood, she had been irresistibly drawn to the dark potency of Charles Savage's intimidating masculinity. But, unlike the others, she hadn't grown out of it, found a man more easily tamed.

She, blind fool that she was, had believed she could handle the forceful and dangerous masculinity she sensed in him, could tame that dark presence with the strength of her love. And despite all that had happened, everything she knew, she had clung to that hopeless belief right up until half an hour ago. Fool!

At last, subsiding breathlessly into her car, she hauled herself together. Zanna knew, and had always known, that only a woman as powerfully seductive, as wilful as she was, could carve a place for herself in Charles's heart—carve it and keep it.

And now she, Beth, knew it too. And, at last, finally and with no looking back, accepted it. She would show the world that she was capable of living without him, could handle her life and her future— no matter how empty it seemed.

The rest of her life began right here and, no matter how tough the exercise, she would never look back.

Her hand quite steady, her features set, she reached for the ignition . . .

CHAPTER FIVE

THE August heat was stifling, thunder brewing ominously. Beth pushed her overlong fringe out of her eyes and tried to concentrate on transcribing her shorthand. She would have to make the effort to drive into Boulogne to get her hair restyled; the normally sleek and elegant cut was growing out of hand.

But what did it matter? she thought tiredly, closing her eyes, her shoulders slumping. Her brave intention to get on with her life, never looking back over her shoulder, had suffered a fatal set-back. How could she avoid staring back into the past when, two days ago, she had discovered she was pregnant?

Two days of remembering that afternoon, over six weeks ago, when her child had been conceived. Two whole days of alternating between the incredulous joy of knowing that her body harboured a brand-new life, a precious life, created with the man she loved, that the fear that the accident had impaired her ability to conceive had been unfounded, and the consequent despair that came of knowing that it was all too late.

Charles already had a child, a son he had welcomed and acknowledged, the woman he had never stopped loving with a passion that amounted to obsession ready and willing to take her place as his second wife.

Which left her, Beth, where?

In an extremely difficult situation.

Her parents would be returning from that world cruise by the middle of next month, and, although they would be saddened by the news of her impending divorce, they would be understanding and supportive. But she could hardly stay at her parents' home, waiting for the birth of her child, while, a scant quarter of a mile away, Charles, his new wife and their son were settling in at South Park. It would put them all in an impossible situation. A situation she couldn't face.

'Are you all right?'

Beth recognised the rough concern in William's voice and opened her eyes, straightening up over her work, feeling guilty.

'I'm fine. Just hot.' She gave him a tight smile. Lately, she had kept her smiles to a sparing minimum, tried to make their relationship more formal. Charles had seen what she had not—that William was more interested in her as a woman than as a secretary.

But then, she excused herself wearily, her love for Charles had been so staunch for so many years that it had blinkered her to the rest of the male sex.

'We're in for a storm.' He came to stand behind her, putting his hands lightly on her shoulders, and she felt her whole body tighten with rejection.

He was a highly intelligent man, a considerate and kindly employer, and he would make some woman an excellent husband. But she wasn't that woman. Her feminine intuition had picked up enough vibes to warn her that he thought she might be. He was an honourable man, not the type to want an affair. And, recently, her eyes had been opened, had seen what Charles had so quickly assimilated. It was all there, if one had the wits to look for it—the way his face lit up when she walked into a room, the way his eyes lingered on her lips, the way he touched her when there was no need to do so. As now.

She shifted abruptly, uneasily, in her seat, and his hands fell away immediately, but he told her quickly, 'Leave that. There's no rush to get it off. My publishers don't set deadlines.'

He moved to the other side of the room, and even though her back was to him she could hear him fiddling with the papers on his desk and her eyes stayed glued to the pages of shorthand waiting to be transcribed into neatly typed manuscript form.

His current book was finished, apart from the few pages to be typed, and when that was done her job here would be over and she would be free to go, and, although she had found security here, of a kind, she couldn't wait. She had her future life to sort out, not to mention that of her unborn child, and she needed to be alone, completely unpressured, before she could decide how best she could support herself and her baby.

'It's far too hot to work,' he mumbled from the other side of the room and then, more briskly, 'Besides, it's almost time for dinner. Mariette left cold beef and salad. Why don't you go and freshen up?'

And as she got to her feet, about to cry off dinner, plead a headache as an excuse for a really early night, he forestalled her. 'Your temporary job here is coming to an end. I'd like to discuss that with you over dinner.'

'Of course.' She covered the typewriter and walked to the door, her clothes sticking to her in the sultry heat. He was, first and foremost, her employer. If he wanted to discuss the termination of her job then she had no right to refuse him.

A generous employer, too, she reflected as, ten minutes later, she stood gratefully beneath a cool shower in her own tiny bathroom. She had saved most of the excellent salary he'd paid her, and she knew how to live frugally—which she would do when she was back in England and looking for work which would enable her to provide for both herself and her baby.

It wouldn't be easy, she thought as she patted herself dry and pulled a loose-fitting light cotton dress over her scanty underwear, fastening the buttons that went all the way down the front. Although it was designed to be belted, she opted to leave the filmy garment loose. It was too close and sultry to be constricted by anything remotely tight.

William probably wanted her to stay on until the end of the week, for although the remainder of the typing would only take another few hours there was always the chance that, having read through it, he might decide to make a few minor alterations. And that would suit her fine, she thought as she walked back into the main house, astonished to find that William had already set the table and brought the cold food from the fridge.

Not a huge or daunting task, she knew, and her soft mouth curved in an amused smile. But William was old-fashioned, and he liked to make himself appear incompetent where anything smacking of domesticity was concerned. Mariette was paid to put his meals in front of him and, on the rare occasion when she left early, that task fell to Beth.

'You look beautifully cool.' The appreciation in his voice as he looked at her from the other side of the room made Beth curse herself for her unguarded smile. Over the past few weeks, when her eyes had been opened at last to his growing awareness of her as a woman, she had been careful to keep everything formal, on a very businesslike footing indeed.

Not that she was apprehensive about it; she wasn't. He wouldn't make a move, say anything out of place, without encouragement. She was quite sure he wasn't that type of man. And encouragement she most definitely wasn't going to give. So she said tonelessly, 'Appearances can be deceptive. I just wish the storm would break to clear the air. I'm practically melting.'

'I've got just the cure for that!' William rubbed his hands, looking pleased with himself. 'Champagne on ice. Just the ticket, wouldn't you say?'

Without waiting for a reply, he filled two flutes, the liquid foaming, spilling on to the carpet, then handed one to Beth, and stood awkwardly, licking the drops from his fingers.

She sat down on the sofa, setting the glass aside. She didn't want the drink; alcohol would turn the niggling ache at the back of her eyes into a full-blown headache. Besides, she was only here with him now to discuss the termination of her part-time employment. So she asked him, 'When are you expecting me to leave? Would the end of the week suit you?'

The remainder of the typing would take a mere hour or so, and that would give her four whole days to make any alterations he might require, pack her gear, and decide how to tackle her future. Four days to get herself ready to leave the relative safety of this peaceful backwater cocoon.

'That's what I wanted to talk to you about.' He sat beside her, a little too close for her liking. He looked ill at ease, running a forefinger round the inside of his shirt collar. 'When my previous secretary ran out on me I immediately got in touch with an agency which specialises in placing people in full-time employment. And now, it seems, they've come up with someone who fits the requirements I laid down at the time. Fiftyish, a dedicated spinster, very efficient, no family ties to speak of, willing to live and work in France and able to start in the autumn when I'm due to begin my next book.'

'Great.' Beth was pleased for him. He was one of the nicest men she had ever met and deserved to have things run smoothly for him. He led a peaceful, uncomplicated life, rarely socialising, his head full of plots and words, leaving little room for anything else.

'Well——'

He didn't seem over the moon about the prospect, Beth noted. His thick brows were drawn together in a frown and his forehead was wet with sweat. Though that, of course, wasn't surprising, she thought wryly. The air inside the little room was like a hot wet blanket.

Outside, thunder cracked violently, making her flinch, lightning illuminating the room for one electrified second, and William mopped his brow with his shirt-sleeve.

'That sounded close. Not frightened, are you?'

'No.' The only thing that frightened her, scared her silly, was the prospect of carrying the burden of her love for Charles through the remainder of her life. Resolutely, she pushed that bitter little reflection out of her head, shrugging. 'Should we eat? It's getting late.'

Not that she was hungry; she wasn't. But she craved solitude, the time needed to work out her future, and as far as she was concerned the discussion was over.

William had found himself an admirable full-time replacement and, although he hadn't said so, she was taking it for granted that she would be free to go at the end of the week.

But he said heavily, 'I'm not happy about your going. I'm sure the woman the agency came up with is admirable, but I'd rather you stayed. Permanently. Would you?'

He was perched on the edge of the seat, his eyes pleading directly into hers, his hands knotted together between his knees, looking as if he was waiting for a decision which would affect the rest of his life.

Beth sighed. A few weeks ago she would have jumped at his offer. The work was stimulating, her surroundings idyllic, the pay more than she felt she deserved and the man himself a poppet. But that had been before she had seen the way he looked at her, before she had realised that he was seeing her as more than a secretary. Before she had discovered she was pregnant.

'Would you?' he repeated thickly. 'And I do mean permanently——' The rest of his words were drowned under another crack of thunder, lashing above them and retreating to rattle among the hills, and the rain came down in torrents, flailing against the walls and windows, and William's face was knotted with frustration as he raised his voice to shout above the fury of the storm,

'I'm asking you to marry me, Beth. As soon as your divorce comes through we'll——'

'You can forget that, Templeton.' The steely, incisive voice made Beth's heart stand still and the room went quiet, and cold. It was as if Charles carried his own atmosphere around with him; even the tumult of the storm seemed to have abated, obliterated beneath the greater, icier violence of his tightly controlled rage.

He was standing in the open doorway, his black, rain-wet hair slicked to his skull, water darkening the fabric of his blue denim shirt, plastering it to the lean hard masculine frame. And he said, his narrowed gunfighter's eyes pinning William to his seat,

'I did knock, but got no reply. You were both, obviously, heavily otherwise occupied.' The steel-grey eyes slid to Beth, making an assessment of the filmy garment she wore, the long level look an insult in itself, and her own eyes dropped as she felt the hectic onslaught of painful colour flood her face.

He could put what interpretation he liked on the scene he had walked in on, and they wouldn't have heard him knock, would they? In the rage of the storm they wouldn't have heard a bomb if it had exploded on the doorstep! But her mind was out of control, her thoughts too chaotic to put into words. She was still in shock, booted there by his unexpected and unwelcome arrival. And it was the bemused William who found his tongue first.

'What do you want?' It wasn't said graciously and he didn't look gracious, his face red with frowning annoyance.

And Charles said simply, his voice curtly precise, 'My wife.'

Beth shuddered uncontrollably. She had never known he had a streak of possessiveness that was so wide and went so deep. He had no further use for her himself, and yet his pride wouldn't allow him to stand by and see another man pursue her. The knowledge made her cold.

'I'm sorry if you find the idea so repellent.' He had noted her shudder, of course he had. He didn't miss a trick. And he went on, the severely honed features demonic, 'But you are my wife. That is a fact.'

'But for how long?' Beth demanded thickly, fighting back. He had heard William's talk of marriage—after the divorce—and had decided, despotically, to nip that little notion in the bud, disregarding the fact that his impatience for his own second marriage had to be the foremost thought in his mind.

He wasn't to know that, even if she weren't pregnant by him, she would never have accepted William's proposal. How could she have done when the cruel fates had conspired to ensure that she would travel through life capable of loving only one man?

He disregarded her throaty question—it had probably hit too closely to home—and his voice was terse with a still, devastating command as he bit out, 'Get packed. We're leaving now.'

His statement hung on the sultry air, suspended by sheer disbelief, and Beth grated out, her nerves at screaming pitch, 'Legally, I may still be your wife. But you can't tell me what to do!' Shaking inside, she made the effort to gather herself together, stay calm. 'I have a job to do here, remember?'

And William, taking his cue from her, blustered, 'That's right, Savage! Beth is employed by me, and paid by me. She has unfinished secretarial duties——'

'Is that what you call them?' Charles queried contemptuously, then went on to tell him, his narrowed, steely eyes never moving from Beth's anguished features, 'The day after tomorrow I'll have a secretary on your doorstep. At my expense, she will finish whatever my wife has left undone. Any other leisure-time projects you might have in mind, Templeton——' his hard mouth curled scornfully '—will be left to her discretion. Now, get your things together, Beth, or leave without them. It's up to you.'

Although his control hadn't flickered by as much as a hair's breadth, Beth knew him well enough to judge the extent of his anger. Knew that at any moment his tightly reined rage could explode with devastating results.

It was there for anyone with the wits to see it, there in the white-knuckled fists bunched against the black fabric that moulded his taut thighs, there in the smoky glint in those normally inscrutable

gunfighter's eyes, in the aggressive tightening of his
hard, wide jawline.

But William hadn't the wits or the discretion to
see that, as far as Charles Savage was concerned,
he was simply someone who was in the way,
someone to be trampled heedlessly underfoot if
necessary, and Beth tensed with apprehension as
her employer got to his feet, blustering, 'Now look
here—you can't barge into my home and tell my
secretary what to do. She may be your wife——' his
face went purple under the shaft of icy contempt
coming his way from the younger, powerfully
leashed intruder '—but, I can tell you this, she
doesn't want you, she wants a divorce. And I'm
not going to stand by and let you force her to do
anything she doesn't want to do.'

The blustering bravado of his tone had drained
away, his voice tailing off, and Beth knew he was
already regretting his hasty defence of her by the
way he suddenly sat down under the frozen threat
of Charles's eyes. And when Charles warned, 'Try
to interfere in my life, and you'll find yourself plastered on the walls,' Beth stalked to the door, her
body rigid with tension because she knew he meant
every word.

She paused, looking back at William, who refused to meet her eyes and dropped his gaze to the
floor. 'I'm sorry. I never had any intention of allowing you to become embroiled in my domestic
concerns. I'll pack now. It's for the best.'

She made her way to her room, her legs stiff, as
if her body was in shock, and gathered her things
together, hurling them haphazardly into her
suitcase. Pummelling them down with her tight little

fists to make them fit, she knelt to fasten the clasps and the light went out, lightning hitting a power line somewhere, knocking out the supply. And that dark voice said from the doorway, almost politely, 'Do you need any help?'

'No!' she said quickly, and then her breath locked in her lungs. She couldn't see him, only sense his dark presence, like a nightmare, every last cell in her body totally and utterly aware of his nearness, and if he came closer she would scream.

Near or far, he represented a danger she could no longer hope to handle. Once she had believed in the power of her love, but that was futile now. It hadn't worked, and never would, and his draconian pursuit of her, his need to bring her to heel, was scaring her out of her wits.

But she wasn't going to let him see that. The one gain from their separation had been in the area of her pride, her self-respect. And she stood up, holding the suitcase in front of her like a shield, her voice tight with the outrage of what he was doing to her, what he was making her endure.

'You had no right to force your way in here, throwing your weight around. Apart from being the height of bad manners, you made me feel cheap, tawdry.'

'I have every right when I hear another man proposing marriage to my wife. I told you I'd be back, and if you feel cheap and tawdry then maybe that's down to the liberties you've been allowing Templeton to take over the last few weeks.'

His voice came thickly through the enveloping darkness, more oppressive than the storm-laden atmosphere, and the thunder growled and prowled, a fitting accompaniment, and she bit down on her lip, ignoring that disgusting insult, because who was he to dish out abuse when he was no doubt thoroughly enjoying an intimate relationship with the woman he intended to make his second wife? She hurled at him instead, 'OK, so you said you'd be back. I've been shaking in my shoes! So what took you so long?'

As if she didn't know! Why should he tear himself away from his south of France romantic interlude with the bewitching Zanna, the company of his child, to bother with his redundant wife? And why he had bothered to turn up eventually she would never know, unless it was to demonstrate how well he could wield the big stick!

'I doubt if the explanations would interest you,' he told her drily. 'You have shown yourself to be remarkably short on interest and concern—except for yourself.'

And she was still trying to get over the gross unfairness of that taunt when lightning jagged through the sky, throwing the grim lines of his devilish features into sharp relief, and he stepped forward, silently covering the space between them, one hand wrenching the suitcase from her, the other taking her arm, his grip inescapable.

'Let's go. I can think of better places to talk this through.'

In the darkness he was too close and Beth's blood thundered, the storm inside her outstripping the storm beyond the stout farmhouse walls. It was difficult negotiating their way through the house in the thick blackness, but Beth wasn't thinking about

that, every sense, every thought unwillingly con-
centrated on the man at her side.

And once, as she blundered into the kitchen table,
he slid an iron-hard arm around her, hauling her
back against the tense warmth of his body.

Beth gave an agonised gasp, the effect of being
so close to him again, her body melting into his as
if they were two parts of a whole, hurting her more
than her painful collision with the edge of the table.

But after a brief, smothered expletive, he moved
on, taking her with him, and because they were so
close she could feel the hammerbeats of his heart,
hear his rapid breathing. Even so, he seemed able
to see in the dark, like a cat, in spite of his being
in unfamiliar surroundings, and when he released
her to drag open the door that led to the courtyard
she sagged against the old oak frame, pulling in
lungfuls of the rain-sweet air.

And only then did her thought processes come
together sufficiently to enable her to ask the
question that should have been uppermost in her
mind, but hadn't been.

'Where are we going? And why?' Why insist on
taking her away from here when everything could
have been dealt with by solicitors? And he surely
didn't want her back at South Park when he would
be taking Zanna and Harry there as soon as the
divorce came through.

And his terse answer bore that out.

'Nowhere you know. Just a place I've found
where we can settle this without interruptions, other
people.'

There was little point in arguing. What could she
say? That she refused to budge an inch? That would

precipitate another scene, drenched with unspoken violence. And she couldn't do that to William. This was his home and this was her problem.

'No squeals of protest?' he enquired witheringly. 'You surprise me.' He took her arm and hustled her out into the rain, his breath hissing, 'No doubt you realise that it's no use running to Templeton for help. Your brave suitor has already thrown in the towel.'

His taunt infuriated her. She was simmering furiously as he hauled her along, her feet splashing through the puddles, the rain stinging her face, plastering her flimsy dress to her body. Who was he to jeer at the older man? William was decent and kind; he would never treat a woman the way Charles had treated her. And no man in his right mind would stand up to Charles Savage in this murderous mood, so his sarcasm, his taunt about throwing in the towel, were out of line.

And as they reached his car she told him so, wrenching her arm from his punishing grasp and informing him roughly, 'William is twice the man you'll ever be; he's——'

'I really don't want to know,' he drawled in return. 'Just get in.'

Which, helped by an ungentle shove from behind, Beth accomplished in seconds and, dripping wet, fuming, sat rigidly in the passenger-seat while the rain lashed the windscreen and Charles tossed her case into the boot before getting in beside her.

Wordlessly, he removed his sodden shirt and threw it on to the back seat, then, flicking on the courtesy light, he turned to her, his face all hard lines, instructing, 'Take your dress off.'

'No.' She started to shiver but felt her body go hot, remembering all too vividly that episode in the woods when their child had been conceived, knowing that her defences against him were all too few, and very tottery. She was already painfully aware of his semi-nudity, the hair-roughened skin covering hard muscle and bone, the almost over-powering need to touch, to run her fingers over the wide thrust of his shoulders, trace the tight nipples with the tips of her fingers and follow the thick hairline to where it disappeared intriguingly beneath the low waistband of his jeans.

And he told her with quiet menace, 'Take it off, or I'll do it for you.' And he meant it, he meant it all right, and there was a sob in her throat, choking her, as her shaking fingers went slowly to the top button nestling between her breasts.

'And you can stop looking like a petrified virgin, my dear. I have no lustful intentions, believe me. I don't want you coming down with pneumonia, that's all.' He reached over to the back and hauled up a car blanket. 'You can placate your modesty with this.' His mouth was cruel as he lashed, 'I've seen your naked body before, remember? And right now I'm not in the mood to feel remotely interested.'

That should have reassured her, but it didn't. How could it when those narrowed, steel-grey eyes watched her every movement as she undid buttons and wriggled out of the clinging wet fabric, fastening on the betraying peaks of her breasts as they flaunted their shaming arousal through the delicate lace of her bra?

And when she made a shaky grab for the rug, to hide herself and the all-too obvious signs of her arousal, he held it back, his voice raw as he commanded roughly, 'And the rest.' But she couldn't move. How could she when her whole body was turning to boneless, aching receptivity, burning for his hands and mouth to touch her as his eyes were doing?

She made a small mew of distress, her pulses going into overdrive. She didn't know which was worse, her self-disgust or knowing that he had to be fully aware of how much she still wanted him. And he made an impatient sound, low in his throat, and swiftly dealt with the front fastening of her bra, his knuckles brushing against the hard, rosy velvet of her nipples before his hands slid to her rounded hips, dragging the matching lacy briefs down the length of her slender legs, his burning eyes resting for one tormenting moment on the riot of darkness that covered her throbbing womanhood before he tossed the rug over her.

'Cover yourself.' His voice was abrasive. And she whimpered, doing just that, shrinking into the soft fabric, hating herself for the way he made her feel, for the way he could so easily make her betray herself. Hating him, too, when he started the engine and asked, almost academically, 'Did you turn on so easily for Templeton? Was that the way you got him begging you to marry him?'

A hard lump of anger pushed against the inside of her chest and she could have wept, but she didn't. Instead, as the headlights of the powerful car cut a glittering swath through the darkness, she told him forcefully, hating him at that moment more than she'd ever hated anyone or anything before, 'You disgust me! You know nothing about my relationship with William. You know nothing! Do you hear me?'

'Oh, I hear you,' he countered rawly, swinging the big car on to the wet surface of the meandering lane. 'And getting to know all about your relationship with Templeton—among other things— is exactly what I have in mind. And where we are going, we'll have all the time it takes. And there won't be another man in miles for you to practise your seductive wiles on. Except me.'

And that was a promise she could do without.

CHAPTER SIX

'WHAT is this place?'

They had been driving for about an hour, the last quarter of which had been spent negotiating a roughly made forest track, straight as a die and probably a firebreak, and now the headlights revealed a small building huddled at the centre of a clearing, the tall trees crowding on every side.

'A shack,' he told her drily. 'Rented and basic it may be, but you may look on it as your temporary home.'

The dim green light from the dash made his face look unearthly, carved from some alien lunar stone and, to counter the terrifying feeling that she no longer knew him at all, had never truly known him or realised just what he was capable of, she snipped back sarcasticaly, 'Gee—thanks! What have I done to deserve such a treat?' ending tartly, 'Where are Zanna and Harry?' Not here, for sure. Charles might have proved himself willing to do anything for the woman he loved, go to the ends of the earth, but the sophisticated Zanna wouldn't spend a moment under the roof of a hovel in the heart of a forest, miles from anywhere.

'Where the hell do you think?' he bit back tersely, the underbrow look he shot her saying he thought her mad, or despicable. Or both.

Beth shrugged, huddling deeper into the rug. His reply told her nothing, of course. He hadn't meant it to. But she could guess. Living the life of Riley in some top international hotel in the south while Zanna waited for him to complete any unfinished business he had with his wife.

She shuddered then, beginning to panic as she wondered what that business would be. Everything could have been dealt with in a civilised way, through solicitors. Why his need to drag her here, subject her to the torment of being near him?

And the panic became almost uncontrollable as he cut the engine and headlights. The darkness was thick, impenetrable, the only sound the pattering of her heartbeats. She was sure he must be able to hear it, able, too, to read the chaos and confusion of her thoughts. But he pocketed the ignition key and told her, 'Stay where you are while I open the place up,' and she was able to breathe more easily as his dark form disappeared into the enveloping blackness. And by the time she saw the orange glow of light shining out from one of the tiny windows she had herself more or less under control.

If she'd been working for a woman, or if Charles hadn't seen what she'd been too blinkered to notice regarding the way William was beginning to feel about her, then he wouldn't have gone to these lengths in order to discuss their pending divorce. She would never have believed his possessiveness to be so deeply ingrained that it extended to the wife he no longer wanted if she hadn't borne the brunt of it.

Having sorted that out, she felt less confused, more able to face the coming twenty-four hours. Whatever it was Charles wanted to discuss with her personally couldn't take longer than that and he

would be anxious to rejoin Zanna and their son.
And the only way to handle what was to come was
to behave with dignity, use her common sense and
try to hide the way she was hurting.

Beginning right now.

Clutching the rug tightly around her, she opened
the car door and slid out her long, naked legs.
Thankfully, it had stopped raining, but she could
still hear the storm grumbling away in the distance,
a dark counterpoint to the steady drip-drip of rain-
drops from the eaves of the forest, and she had
only gone two slithery paces towards the little light
from the cottage when Charles appeared as if out
of nowhere, his tall shadowy figure forbidding.

'Where the hell do you think you're going?'

His sudden, silent appearance had shocked the
breath out of her lungs, making her doubt her
ability to handle this at all, but pride came to her
rescue again, had her hauling herself together,
helping her to inject a note of sarcasm as she flung
back witheringly, 'Out on the town, where else?'
and made to walk past him, heading for that square
of orange light, but he muttered a harsh expletive
and scooped her up into his arms and she pum-
melled furiously against the hard bones of his
shoulders, yelping,

'Put me down. I am capable of walking a few
yards!' Being held so very close to him was seriously
undermining her mental stability, she told herself,
cursing the fragility of her resolve where he was
concerned. This close she could easily find herself
melting against him, all liquid invitation, begging
him to allow her to try, once again, to teach him
to love her.

'Suit yourself. If you want to wade through ankle-deep mud, so be it,' he snapped out, then slid her down the length of his body which, she decided in miserable confusion, rated even higher in erotic stimulation than being carried in his arms.

Biting her lip, she watched him stride ahead of her, sure-footed as a cat. What did she have to do to turn the tide of her emotions? How could she stop loving him, wanting him, and begin the long haul back to the peace of mind she craved?

Unable to find the answer, fearing she never would, she began to follow, ignoring the drag of mud, intent only on staying on her feet now, keeping the rug tightly wrapped around her body.

'The power's out,' he informed her curtly as she stepped over the threshold and closed the thick plank door behind her. And, rather than look at him, meet those clever, steely eyes, she peered about her.

It was a small room, the stone tiles beneath her feet cracked and uneven with age, the walls roughly plastered, painted white, the furniture mostly pine, cottage antiques. There were logs laid in the open hearth ready for firing, and the two oil-lamps he had lit cast a warm, intimate glow. A narrow wooden staircase led up from one corner of the room and he must have been following the direction of the assessment she had tried to make appear cool and only vaguely interested because he told her acidly,

'We have two rooms. This and the bedroom above. The kitchen and bathroom are tacked on. Primitive, but adequate. I imagine it was once a woodsman's hut; it's not large enough to have been a hunting lodge.'

'I can't imagine why you bothered.' A nice touch of derision there. She bent to remove her muddy shoes, careful to keep her grasp on the enveloping rug firm, still keeping her eyes averted from him, then padded past him, making a show of opening the door which led into the built-on kitchen.

Basic, as he had said, but, as they wouldn't be here for more than a few hours tomorrow, adequate enough. And then, because she could sense his eyes on her, watching her every movement, she told him coldly, 'If, for some unknown reason, you wanted to discuss the details of the divorce personally, instead of through solicitors, you could have done it by phone. Don't you think dragging me out here was a touch melodramatic?' Oh, nicely said, she congratulated herself hollowly. She was at last getting the hang of presenting a cool, almost disinterested façade around him.

But the small success didn't make her feel any better; worse, if anything. She heard the deep pull of his indrawn breath and she did look at him then, hoping there was no trace of her inner anguish in her eyes. And what she saw made her heart turn over because he looked like a man who had recently travelled to hell.

His skin was taut across his facial bones, the character lines more deeply drawn, and there was a brooding savagery in his eyes that she had only seen once before. And that had been when Zanna had left him that first time.

First time? She shook her head unconsciously, pushing that unbelievable thought aside. She dared not allow herself to believe that the woman he loved, always would love, had once again walked out on him. But why else should he look as though the light had gone out of his life?

And then the moment was gone, pushed away by his tempered steel voice. 'And left you happily where you were—enjoying Templeton's love-making, drawing up cosy little plans for when you could be married? Sorry, my dear,' his voice became a menacing drawl, 'but I don't operate that way. And neither, as my wife, do you.'

Pointless to remind him that she wouldn't be his wife for much longer, or to tell him that William had never made love to her, that she would have run a mile if he'd tried it. That he might have proposed but that she would never have accepted in a million years. Pointless.

Suddenly Beth felt tears sting at the back of her eyes, making her throat burn. And she felt incredibly weary of the whole sorry mess, incredibly tired. She said numbly, 'If it's all the same to you, I'd like to get out of this rug,' then wished she'd kept her mouth firmly closed, a slow burn of colour covering her face as she remembered the way he'd looked at her naked body when, at his insistence, she'd removed her sodden clothing. Recalled how he'd asked if she turned on as easily for William. He must think she was a sex-starved tramp.

Besides, he had to remember her passionate, uninhibited response to his lovemaking before the loss of their child. The way he had refused to come near her, touch her, in the empty months that had followed. He would be putting two and two together and drawing the conclusion that sexual frustration

had led her to jump into bed with William
Templeton, not to mention wholeheartedly enjoying a sexual romp on the floor of the forest with
the husband she had professed not to want, had
walked out on!

His face was white, his mouth clamped in tight
disgust, a muscle working sporadically along his
hard jawline and, to dispel what he was obviously
thinking, she said sharply, 'Don't worry, I'm not
offering anything. I'd simply like to have a hot bath,
if there is such a thing, and turn in. Whatever you
have to say to me can wait until tomorrow.'

He didn't say a word. He gave her a long, complicated look then picked up her suitcase and walked
up the narrow stairs. Beth followed, reluctantly and
only because she had to, had no other option,
clutching at the rug, hoisting it above her knees,
afraid she might trip.

The stairs gave directly into a bedroom with a
sloping ceiling. It was basically and simply fur-
nished with a double bed she thought she might
need a step-ladder to climb on to, a pine chest of
drawers and a chair, and no door except one in
narrow, white-painted pine boards, set into the op-
posite wall.

'The bathroom, such as it is, is through there.'
Charles put the case down and gestured towards
the white-painted door. 'No bath, but there is a
shower and if the power's gone out recently there
should still be some hot water.' He turned and took
a dark navy sweater from one of the drawers,
pulling it over his head.

She snapped out, all too revealing, 'About time,
too!' Half naked, he presented a problem, es-

pecially so in the confines of the small room. She only had to look at his bronzed, hair-roughened skin to ache to touch it, to feel the vital warmth of flesh and blood, the hardness of bone and sinew, to feel his body respond to her as once it had done.

And one brow arched darkly, as if he knew what lay behind her snapped retort, but his mouth was unsmiling, the look he gave her long and hard before wide shoulders rose in a slight, dismissive shrug beneath the clinging, expensive wool. 'It's gone colder. I'll put a match to the fire before I make supper. Soup and rolls be enough?'

It had gone colder. The storm had cleared the air and the interior of the cottage felt chilly. Still Beth's slight body was burning, every cell, every nerve-end ignited by the mere fact of his presence, but she wasn't going to admit to that. And she wasn't going to prolong the torment of this crazy evening.

Tomorrow morning, after a night's sleep, would be soon enough to get to grips with his reasons for bringing her here, listen to whatever it was he had to say that couldn't have been discussed by letter or over the phone.

'I don't want anything.' She turned her back, opening her suitcase and rummaging around for the old, worn T-shirt she had taken to wearing to bed since leaving him.

Before then, before that fateful day when Zanna had reappeared, she had always worn the finest satins and silks at night, the most seductive nightwear money could buy, because she had never given up hoping that he would change his mind and come to her...

'Just one thing...' The harshness of his tone made her spine go stiff, her fingers rigid among the muddle of her hurried packing. 'Did you meet up with Templeton before, arrange to leave me and go to him? Or was it sheer coincidence that you went to work for him and made him fall in love with you?'

She did move then. Moved in one swift, fluid movement, totally oblivious of the way the rug pooled at her feet. And her head came up, her eyes sparking emerald defiance, clashing with his icily narrowed, probing gaze.

'Don't tar me with the same brush that blackened you!' Throughout their married life he had secretly yearned for the woman he really loved, had at some stage met up with her, arranged for her, Beth, to be tossed aside like an old rag. Must have done. Zanna had already known that his marriage was over. He had to have told her. Had he pleaded with Zanna to return to him, promised to get rid of his unwanted wife?

'Talk about double standards!' she spluttered on, furious now, forgetting her vow to remain calm, in control, act as if she no longer cared, had stopped caring a long time ago. 'But no, I had never met William before I went to work for him. And no again, I didn't "make" him fall in love with me.'

She was in a prime position to know how cold-bloodedly he'd married her, making no secret about his desire for a family, young children to fill the empty rooms at South Park, to inherit his considerable wealth. He had never even pretended to love her. Simply decided, after that six months' probationary period, that she would make an acceptable mother of his children, a good hostess, a biddable wife. So, knowing all that, she couldn't help tacking on, her short upper lip curling scornfully, 'Do you really see me as the sort of woman who could go around seducing every man she meets into falling in love?'

The very idea was risible, insane, and Charles was at last showing himself in his true colours, revealing the tortuous reasoning behind his strange behaviour.

He hadn't followed her to France to discuss their divorce, dragged her here because he had some complicated settlement to talk out. The cunning devil was trying to turn the tables, to make her seem the guilty party. How he must have rubbed his hands when he'd walked in and witnessed William's proposal of marriage!

He was sneaky and devious and——

And he was looking at her, a small smile tugging at the corners of his mouth, his eyes caressing her heaving breasts, sliding over her narrow waist, the gentle curve of her belly, down her long, slender legs, then slowly up again. And the smile became very slightly cruel as he told her, 'Very capable indeed. Capable of seducing any man who's once looked on that delectable body and is fool enough to think he can hold on to you.'

And only then, at last penetrating her fury, came the knowledge that she was stark naked!

She swooped, almost toppling over in her panic, her fingers scrabbling for the protective covering she hadn't, in her blind anger, realised she'd lost, dragging it up in front of her, colour scalding her face.

And when her stormy eyes at last locked with his she was sure she could detect the cruel light of amusement in the stony depths, and he said, slowly and very deliberately, 'That's one thing straight. Something we can begin to work on tomorrow.' Then turned on his heels. And although she couldn't make sense of what he had said she could swear she could hear his silent, derisive laughter ringing inside her head as he went swiftly down the stairs.

As soon as he'd gone she made a determined effort to pull herself together and began to hurry. She wouldn't put it past him to come back up, and having him walk in on her while she was in the shower was something she could do without.

Thankfully, he'd left the lamp he'd carried upstairs and as she put it down carefully on a marble-topped washstand in the tiny bathroom she reflected that he might also decide to share her bed. The thought made her go cold.

They hadn't shared a bed since her miscarriage and if he decided he wouldn't be able to sleep on the small, hard-looking sofa downstairs and took it into his head to join her she didn't know what she would do.

Throw him out? Physically, she was no match for him and if he'd made up his mind there would be nothing she could do or say to make him change it. And if she tried to leave him to it, sleep on the uncomfortable sofa herself, he would be angry and she knew what could happen then.

It was anger, nothing less, that had sparked off his arrogant male desire that afternoon in the forest ... And her control was still too fragile to be relied on ...

He hadn't been near her. Which shouldn't have surprised her, given his track record during the latter part of their marriage. But it did, she thought, struggling into a sitting position, her knees up to her chin, the duvet huddled around her.

Or was it disappointment? asked a snide little voice from deep inside her. But she pushed the notion away, quickly. No, of course not. If he'd joined her in bed she'd been planning on feigning sleep but knew that if he so much as touched her—even accidentally—she would have jumped like a scalded cat or melted straight into his arms. Either way, the ending would have been the same.

And although having him make love to her would be nothing short of ecstasy it would also be a massive stumbling-block where her resolve to get on with her life without him, never looking back, was concerned.

Besides, on his part, it would only be animal lust. He didn't love her, never had. He'd never stopped loving Zanna. So, it would be lust, allied to his desire to stamp her in his own mind as a tramp, always willing, whatever the occasion, whoever the man!

She was quite sure now that he was intent on making her out to be the guilty party, finding all the evidence he could to point to that—hence the lovemaking on the first occasion he'd tracked her down. She could be turned on by anyone—the first man she'd come into contact with after leaving, the man who happened to be her employer—even the husband she'd asked for a divorce only had to touch her to get her half crazed with desire, begging for more!

Oh, yes, she thought sourly, running her fingers through her rumpled hair, she knew he intended making her out to be a shameless tramp, the guilty party in the break-up of their marriage. And, what was more, she knew why!

The Savage family had been at South Park for generations, owning most of the land, most of the property, for miles around. They were looked up to, almost revered as good landlords, local squires noted for their compassion and concern, interested in the lives and problems of the village and surrounding scattered-farm population.

Reciprocally, the community returned that interest, and with a vengeance! Nothing the Savage family did escaped the notice of at least one villager, who would then proceed to pass it on to everyone willing to listen. And most were more than willing, although her father had once grunted, 'Gossip may be a normal human failing, but this time it's going too far. I pity the poor devil, having to lead his life in the full glare of public scrutiny and mindless tittle-tattle—he's having a hard enough time, without knowing that every last move he makes is avidly discussed on every doorstep.'

And even now she could still hear her mother's patient reply. 'The gossip isn't malicious. People are sorry for him—especially now that James is working abroad. Poor Charles has simply gone in on himself, shutting himself away in that great empty house, brooding. He was obsessed by that Zanna Hall, everyone knew it. And now she's left him. People say she refused point-blank to marry him and tie hersef down.'

'"People say"!' her father had repeated scathingly. 'They might well say, but how much do they actually know?'

'You'd be surprised.' Her mother had quietly continued with her knitting. 'Anyway, you can't hide something as obvious as an all-out obsession. Everyone said no good would come of it. And it hasn't, has it?'

No, no good had come of it, Beth reflected sourly. And Charles would be perfectly well aware how tongues would wag—with utter disgust this time—if the gossips were to get hold of the information that he'd thrown little Beth Garner-that-was, the respected local GP's daughter, out on her neck to make room for Zanna Hall and their ready-made family. Which was why he would move heaven and earth to make himself seem the injured party! He wouldn't want to lose his standing with the local population, many of whom were his tenants, she decided cynically.

And he seemed to be sleeping late, she thought, swinging her legs over the side of the high, old-fashioned bed. Though how he could do that, on the small, uncomfortable sofa, she hadn't the least idea. But she was utterly thankful that there was no sound of him moving around when, as her feet touched the floor, the familiar morning nausea hit her.

She only just made it to the bathroom in time and emerged ten minutes later, grey-faced, to pull on a pair of well-worn jeans and an emerald-green cotton blouse. After a glass of water and a slice of dry toast she would be fine. Ready to face what the day had in store. That it would be nothing pleasant, she knew full well. But, somehow, she would handle it.

At least Charles hadn't surfaced to witness her violent bout of morning sickness, she consoled herself as she picked her way downstairs. She had no intention of telling him about the child they had conceived. It would smack of emotional blackmail.

If he preferred Zanna, and of course he did, then she wasn't going to use their unborn child as leverage to make him stay with her. The thought of tying him to her, knowing he was in love with someone else, made her feel ill. Besides, he already had a child, a son to carry his name, given him by the woman he had never stopped loving, a son who would soon legitimately bear his name.

It was something she had already accepted and the sooner this day was over and she was free to get on with the rest of her life, the better it would be. And the very first thing to do was to tackle Charles head-on, tell him she knew what he was up to, what he was trying to prove.

And then, she thought, she would tell him to go to hell! Because maybe, just maybe, she was at last beginning to get some sense! How could she possibly love a man who could do that to her? And when they came face to face she would tell him precisely how despicable he was, not worth a moment's thought. And by saying it out loud she might make it the truth.

But easier said than done. A thorough search of the tiny cottage—which didn't take longer than a couple of minutes—told her he wasn't around. And his car had gone.

As she stood in the centre of the clearing, the mud now rapidly drying out in the morning sun, her green eyes clouded with exasperation. Where the hell was he?

And half an hour later she was still asking the same question, but more with anxiety now because surely he wouldn't have gone to the trouble to bring her here, only to disappear into thin air himself?

A sudden thought sent relief spurting through her and she dived for the small fridge, pulling it open then closing it slowly, something more than disappointment making her shoulders slump.

So he hadn't gone to the nearest village for supplies, she thought drearily. The fridge was fully stocked. And he must have spent some time here, she thought, pouring a glass of water and sipping it reflectively. The store cupboards, too, were well stocked with tinned and dried food and she knew he had a few changes of clothing in the drawers upstairs. And it couldn't have been his intention to bring her here and dump her goodness knew how many miles from another human being, no means of transport and no phone!

But worse than that uncomfortable thought—so very much worse—was the tight ache inside her chest that came from missing him! And that knocked her former theory that her pride wouldn't allow her to go on loving him right on the head, didn't it just!

At the sound of a car drawing into the clearing she went weak with relief. He was back! She fled over the room and out through the door, her heart racing. No need to wonder why she suddenly felt so light-hearted, she thought drily, why the relief that he had not, as she had begun to fear, been taken ill in the night and had driven away, looking for medical assistance, was almost intoxicating. She still loved the swine. Her foolish heart refused to listen to the wisdom of her head.

She stood watching him as he got out of the car, his movements relaxed and smooth, and she pushed her hair back out of her eyes. Her hand was shaking. And something of what she was feeling must have got through to him because he walked slowly towards her, stopping, towering right over her, and he said lightly, his mouth curling upwards just a little, 'Missed me?'

Totally unable to deny what she was sure any fool could read on her face, she said thickly, 'Where were you?' and suddenly felt claustrophobic, as if the tall trees were moving nearer, crowding her, smothering her. But it had nothing to do with the forest. He was doing the crowding. He hadn't moved, he hadn't needed to, his very presence was suffocating her.

And there was more than a smile in his eyes right now.

The narrowed grey slits were knowing as they rested for a lingering moment on her wide, shocked green eyes then drifted slowly down, assessing the suddenly soft trembling vulnerability of her parted lips, and down again to the revealing peaks of her breasts as they pushed in aching invitation against the fine cotton of her blouse.

And there wasn't even a hint of a query now as he moved a pace nearer and repeated, a shocking glint of something triumphant, alive and deep in his eyes, 'You missed me.'

She picked up the danger and desperately tried to negate it, shaking her head, her denial too vehement as her pulses suddenly changed gear, racing.

'You're crazy! I thought you'd dumped me. Wondered how far I'd have to walk, dragging a heavy suitcase, before I got back to civilisation—that's all.' Her eyes met his defiantly, impressing the lie, but she saw the soft insolence of his smile and shuddered.

He didn't believe a single word, and the angry reaction to the way she had actually worried about the brute had her snapping out, 'Where the hell were you, anyway?'

'Finding a phone and arranging for one of my secretaries to present herself on your former boss's doorstep to deal with your unfinished professional business.' He laid slight stress on the 'professional' but his shrug was minimal as he moved in, stating, 'It's not important.'

And what was? she wondered chaotically, as those narrowed, steely eyes undressed her, absorbing the fine tremors that invaded her skin. That she had missed him, worried about him? Did he get his kicks out of making her emotions go into a state of aching confusion? Turning her into a gibbering wreck while he stayed so calm, so coolly aloof?

But there was nothing aloof about the slow burn she glimpsed behind his eyes, nothing aloof about the way he brought his hand up, the tanned skin of his long, hard fingers brushing against the peachy softness of her cheek, lingering for one tantalising moment against the fullness of her lips, making them part, revealing her trembling vulnerability.

Oh, nothing aloof at all.

Beth shuddered, watching her control slide out of existence with a strange detachment. He only had to touch her...

Touch her. The warm pads of his fingers were resting now on the tiny pulse that was beating so frantically at the base of her throat and he said thickly, 'You are so beautiful.'

He had never said that to her before and, for a brief space of time, for a few glorious, heady moments, she believed him. Could believe nothing else as his mouth took hers, his strong, inescapable arms drawing her so close to the hard length of his body that they seemed to be fused together, divided only by the thin superfluity of clothing, paradoxically made whole by the very separateness of their sex.

And her senses went haywire as his hands shaped her body, making it blossom beneath the sliding sensuality of his touch.

Greedily, lost in the wanton responsiveness only he could call forth, her body moved against his, soft breasts crushed against the heated masculinity of his chest, hips pressing urgently on to his, the obvious strength of his arousal making her mindless, boneless, utterly receptive. And her head was spinning, her brain functions on hold, as he swept her up into his arms and carried her back to the cottage, his long stride purposeful. And her head fell back against the taut breadth of his shoulder, her lazy eyes sweeping languorously to his profile, and her heart almost exploded with rapacious sensation as the glint of resolve in those predatory, narrowed eyes, the dull flush of naked desire that brushed the taut skin across his angular cheekbones, the sensual curve of that hard, bold mouth told a story that was as old as time...

CHAPTER SEVEN

IN A daze of receptive sensuality, Beth felt as if she were being wafted upstairs on the wings of a dream. In reality, Charles's arms were holding her close, his dark head dipped as his mouth curved erotically over the exposed skin of her long white throat, the delicate angle of her jaw, the sensitive hollow just below her ear. And that was so much better, infinitely more satisfying than any dream.

And a drugging mist of fantasy kept her pinned to the bed, her body so boneless that she felt as if she were drowning in honey, and languorously she became plastic beneath the sureness of his hands, her breath swelling within her as he slowly unbuttoned the green cotton blouse, pulling it away from the gleaming slenderness of her shoulders as if it were a thing of no substance, dissolving in the heated, narcotic sexual tension that throbbed and sighed in the air.

A tension that inexorably began to tighten. She could feel the build-up, the spiralling heat so deep inside her, felt it and caught the echo of it coming from him, calling her, binding her. And as the last of her clothing disappeared beneath the wicked magic of his hands, he straightened, the heat of desire marking the high slash of his cheekbones, the brooding intensity of his eyes holding hers captive as his hands went to the buckle of his belt.

And it couldn't possibly be better, she thought, feeling him leave the bed, hearing the rustle of his clothing, the faint scratchy sound as he dealt with the zip of his jeans. So many times during the long summer morning, so many times, all of them revealing a different aspect of his sexuality—savagely masterful, tender, slow, so slow with the sensuality of the true voluptuary. So many times and all of them beautiful...

A light tap on her naked backside, a tap that almost lingered, hovered, just, and so tantalisingly, on the edge of a new discovery, pulled her out of drugging memory and he said, 'Food. Ten minutes. OK?'

And she simply nodded, on a plane too divorced from reality to speak because that tap had lingered, full of promise—if promises were needed...

Twenty minute later, showered, dressed now in a full filmy cotton skirt with a toning peacock-blue sleeveless blouse tied just beneath her breasts, she wandered down to the tiny kitchen. She still felt disorientated, as if she had beeen drugged, reality blurred and suspended. But her nostrils quivered appreciatively at the aroma of grilled bacon and she said lightly, 'So you mastered the stove. You deserve a medal!'

It was a cranky-looking monster, and ran on bottled gas, and to Beth's jaundiced eye it looked about a thousand years old, but Charles gave her an odd, tight smile, hunched one shoulder and turned to yank at the door of the oven. And she looked at him, weak still with the ecstasy of what had happened, a weakness compounded by what her lingering eyes drank in—the tall, lean strength of him, the wide, rangy shoulders covered in the dark cotton of his shirt, the worn jeans that snuggled to spare hips, neat buttocks and long sexy legs.

But he wasn't looking at her as he extracted two plates from the oven, holding them with a cloth. And he walked quickly over to a ramshackle apology for a breakfast bar which, she saw, he had taken the trouble to spread with a checked table-cloth and had set out with fruit conserves, a crock of butter, a rack of fresh toast and a big brown pot from which he began to pour steaming, fragrant tea.

'I'm starving,' she admitted, pulling up a stool and sitting down to a plate mounded with bacon and mushrooms.

He joined her, picking up his cutlery, and instead of agreeing he said, 'Tell me exactly why you decided to walk out on our marriage.'

It was like being flung into a bath of cold water. It took her breath away and, for a moment, she couldn't reply because they were back to reality again.

And, suddenly, she didn't think she could face it, not the cold, hard reality of him and Zanna and Harry. Yet, staring down at her plate, she knew she had to. What had happened this morning had to be firmly placed right at the back of her mind, along with the consequences of their lovemaking over six weeks ago.

Somehow she was going to have to make a life for herself and the child she was going to bear, and now was the time to start, she informed herself tartly, not feeling too brave about it.

So she said, in what she hoped was a tone of level reasonableness, 'I told you why, before I left. Surely you can't have forgotten.'

She couldn't bring herself to mention Zanna. She had already told him how she'd overheard that damning conversation, and he might begin to put two and two together if she as much as mentioned that woman's name.

Her pride, or what was left of it, demanded that he should believe that she was the one to abandon their marriage. She was not, in his eyes at least, willing to appear as the spurned and discarded wife!

'I haven't forgotten a single damn word,' he replied heavily. Then, 'What I want to know is why. You lacked nothing. We were good together.'

Her mouth tightened, her fingers knotted together in her lap. Did he think that material things counted for anything? Did he want blood? Did he really want her to confess that her already wounded pride had made her leave before he got the opportunity to throw her out? Would his male ego continue to be piqued until he had wrung just such a confession from her? And she snapped at him heatedly, 'Good together? I disagree. For three months you didn't come near me, stayed away more often than not—you couldn't bear to touch me.'

His face was a battleground of warring emotions, the conflict graphically painted in the hard slash of his mouth, the tightness of skin over jutting cheekbones and jaw, the deep dark silver glints in those narrowed, brooding eyes, and she looked at him compulsively, her heart beating heavily because the truth was here, between them, a cruel, cold and hurting thing.

She said quickly, 'You don't really want me. You never did. I got tired of being second-best.' And that was more of the truth than was wise to release. He could pick it up, examine it, and maybe find the knowledge of her long and hopeless love.

But he said rawly, 'I don't know what the hell you're talking about!' and strode over to the stone sink, tipping his unfinished meal into the waste bin. Then he turned and faced her, his shoulders rigid with tension, his eyes hard as he grated out, 'Didn't our recent lovemaking tell you anything about how much I want you?'

Their lovemaking. That beautiful, beautiful phantom happiness. It hurt too much to think about it. And if he looked back on it, too, he would re-cognise her unrestrained responsiveness for what it was, understand how much it revealed about her true feelings for him.

And so she made her face blank, lifted her chin and fixed her gaze on a point just above his head because if she met his eyes she would be defeated utterly, and told him with a tiny dismissive shrug, 'You couldn't bring yourself to touch me during the final months of our marriage—that tells me how much you want me. The other—well——' She schooled the wobble of misery out of her voice, replaced it with a throwaway nonchalance that sur-prised even herself. 'I've already written that off as frustration.'

It wasn't true, of course it wasn't. But it was slightly easier than admitting to the bleak suspicion that he had been simply using her to convince himself of her latent promiscuity.

She expected exasperation, perhaps annoyance, even, over what he would see as a blasé comment. Expected that, but not the white-hot rage which had him covering the small distance between them after one long, deadly moment of silence.

His face was tight with it, those narrowed eyes spitting fire, his hands cruel as he dragged her off her precarious perch on the rickety stool and set her on her feet. And his voice was murderous, low and clipped.

'You little bitch! Just thank your lucky stars I don't hit women.' His hands dropped away abruptly, as if physical contact with her disgusted him. But a stroke of hot colour burned across his high slanting cheekbones as he grated, his voice raw with emotion, 'I didn't touch you because I bloody well couldn't! I was full of guilt. Ridden with it, do you hear me?'

She heard. Oh, she heard. But she didn't understand. She shook her head, stepping back, her face white with misery, and the silence was heavy, thick with things she didn't understand, and she didn't know why he was doing this to them, why he was complicating the dreadful simplicity of his need to be free of one wife to take another.

He said sharply, each word cutting her like a knife, making her change her knowledge of him, of herself and her reactions to him, 'You were expecting our child. You were light with joy, a complete and confident woman.' His mouth twisted in a bitter line. 'And I changed all that. You lost the child and, for all we know, lost the opportunity of conceiving another. And I was behind the wheel.' He swung on his heels, as if unable to look at the beaten creature he believed she had become, and walked to the door.

Beth began to say he mustn't feel guilty, not over that, but the words were stopped in her throat when he whipped round again, facing her, telling her, 'I hired this place for a couple of weeks. I thought we needed and deserved at least that much time to resolve our future.' His voice was toneless now, totally without life, or even, seemingly, interest. 'But now I find I can't wait that long. I can't command the necessary patience and ingenuity to work it through.' He moved out of the door, into a shaft of sudden sunlight, but even that brilliance failed to thaw the ice in his eyes. 'I want you to return to South Park, where, as my wife, you should be. I want no further talk of separations—trial or otherwise—and certainly not of divorce.'

'But what about——?'

'No buts.' He made a slashing gesture with one hand, blocking her tumbling questions about where Zanna and Harry would fit into that particular arrangement. 'It's straightforward enough. Come back to England with me and we'll try to forget the past couple of months ever happened. Or tell me you don't want me at any price. Then we can both wipe the slate clean. I won't beg—I don't even want to. It's entirely your decision, and I want it by tonight.'

He walked away then and Beth stood watching his tall, broad-shouldered figure stride purposefully across the sunlit yard and on to a forest track, the trees swallowing him, taking him away, leaving her feeling more empty and alone than she had ever felt in her life.

Blindly, she walked back into the centre of the small kitchen and began to clear up, hurling her untouched breakfast into the bin, her movements clumsy and uncharacteristically uncoordinated.

No prizes for guessing why Charles had made that ultimatum. Her earlier, and quickly dismissed, idea that Zanna had once again walked out on him had proved to be correct. She could kill the bitch! How dared the hateful creature hurt her darling time and time again?

Then, realising that her feet were planted on the path to hysteria, she took herself in hand and, her soft mouth compressed, gushed a tepid stream from the ineffectual water heater on to the plates in the sink.

Despite everything, she loved Charles. And love could make a fool of the most sensible soul alive. She had been made a fool of once, through loving more deeply than wisely, and it mustn't happen again.

She had to think of herself, acknowledge the impossibility of remaining the wife of a man who was obsessed by another woman. That the other woman was a bitch, incapable of true and abiding love, uncaring of how much torment and pain she inflicted on the father of her child, had nothing to do with the case, she assured herself tightly as she dealt with the breakfast dishes.

Her failure to win his love in the past had taught her a lesson she would be a fool to forget. That their relationship had degenerated abysmally, with little hope of salvation and no hope at all for a return to the civilised and caring thing it had been during the early months of their marriage, had been clearly demonstrated by his ultimatum.

Obviously, with the feckless Zanna out of his reach yet again, he would prefer her to return to South Park and take up her duties as his wife. It would save him from having to face the unsavoury gossip which would undoubtedly follow on a divorce, and, she thought cynically, stowing the last of the cutlery away in a drawer, she had made a career out of being his wife, had been good at the job. Yes, he would prefer her to go back with him but wouldn't much care if she didn't.

Even if she had been tempted to stay married to him, his blunt ultimatum, his careless take-it-or-leave-it attitude, his open admission that he didn't have the patience to try to persuade her—which would entail making love to her at every opportunity until she was utterly seduced into mindless acquiescence—would have put an end to that!

And his insensitive comment about forgetting the past couple of months demonstrated exactly how little he thought of her. How could she ever possibly forget Zanna's return—with their son tucked under her arm—and his obvious desire to get rid of his existing wife in order to marry the woman he couldn't stop loving?

Her chores finished, she wandered outside and sat on a wooden bench near the front door, closing her eyes and allowing the green and golden peace to surround her. She would face her future alone. When Charles came back she would tell him so.

It was all over. Except for one last thing. If they parted tomorrow, or even later tonight, never saw each other again, she had to rid him of those feelings of guilt about the loss of their child.

Slow tears trickled from beneath her closed eyelids, the last she would ever shed for either of them, because if she had known his feelings she wouldn't have felt so worthless and rejected herself, and they could have helped each other through those dreadful days and lonely nights, and the last few months of their ill-fated no-hoper of a marriage would not have spawned the bitter memories they were both going to drag into their separate futures.

CHAPTER EIGHT

BETH was calm, very calm. At least, she thought she was, until Charles walked in on her and every cell in her body went on red alert.

He appeared in the open doorway of the kitchen and he must have walked for miles. His shirt was wet with sweat, sticking to his body, his dark hair damp, unruly, as if he'd pushed his hands through it time and time again. She met the brooding intensity of his eyes and shuddered. He looked exhausted, driven, and her love for him made her tender heart twist in unwilling compassion.

Almost, she was ready to do whatever he asked of her, be whatever he wanted her to be. But only almost. Unconsciously shaking her head, she dismissed the aching temptation. The raw, emotional savagery coming from him had to be down to the pain of having Zanna reject him yet again. It assuredly had nothing to do with whether or not she was willing to forget the divorce she'd told him she wanted.

'We'll eat in half an hour.' The banality of his words was negated utterly by the low harshness of his tone, riven with a pain as dark as it was unknowable, and she nodded mutely, unable to speak, her mouth gone dry, and turned blindly back to the sink where, just before he'd returned, she'd been washing salad.

She heard him move behind her, on his way through to the tiny sitting-room, and felt her whole body tense with her unstoppable, helpless awareness of him. And only when she heard him mount the stairs, heard the sound of his movements in the bathroom overhead, the gush and rattle of the nightmarish plumbing, did she feel herself relax, her body sagging with reaction.

Closing her eyes, she leant against the sink and willed herself to recapture the calm acceptance, the stoicism she had found during the long green and golden day. She wasn't prepared to take second place in his life and she couldn't help him come to terms with what Zanna had done to him. No one could. He would have to call upon his own deep reserves of mental strength to accomplish that. And he, above all men, was strong enough to do it.

Fleetingly, she wondered why the other woman had taken off again. She had seemed determined to replace her as Charles's wife, more than happy with the situation, had agreed that yes, her intention was to legitimise their son, allow him to bear his father's name.

Motherhood had obviously failed to tame the wild and reckless streak that was such a strong part of Zanna Hall's wayward character. She wouldn't be tamed and she wouldn't be caged and she went through life doing exactly as she pleased, utterly regardless of who got hurt in her selfish, flamboyant progress.

Beth pushed herself away from the sink and straightened her shoulders. She refused to think about it any more. She had enough to do to keep herself calm. Telling Charles that she wanted that

divorce was going to require a single-minded
strength of purpose she only hoped she possessed.

She had a meal to produce and she would concentrate on that, but even so the steaks she had
found in the fridge were only just beginning to sizzle
when Charles came down and she shot him a quick,
questioning look—which told her nothing about his
mood, about anything, except that he had
showered, changed into a black cotton sleeveless
T-shirt and hip-hugging denims.

'Anything I can do to help?' he offered blandly.

She made her voice crisp and did her best to look
extremely efficient as she bustled about, spreading
the breakfast bar with the checked cloth, setting
out the bread and the salad, telling him, 'No, not
really. Thanks,' meaning that the only thing he
could do for her was give her permanent amnesia,
make her forget that she had ever met him, ever
loved him.

'In that case, I'll open the wine.' Toneless. Polite.
She wondered frenziedly when he would ask for her
decision, then mentally slammed that enervating
thought out of existence. He would ask when he
was ready and in the meantime there was something she could do for him. One last thing.

She turned the steaks and took the glass of red
wine he held out to her, drank it down in two long
swallows and immediately felt better. Dutch courage
was better than no courage at all, she informed
herself sagely as she reached into the wall cupboard
for the mustard and marmalade.

'Templeton's lavish hand with the champagne
must have given you a taste for the bottle,' he said
drily. 'The most I've ever seen you put back before

is half a glass, and you've made that last all evening.'

Nevertheless, he refilled her glass and she ignored that taunt about the Pol Roger he must have noticed when he'd walked into William's home and dragged her out. It wasn't important. What she had to say to him was.

Forking the steaks on to two plates, she carried them over, sucked in her breath and told him, not quite meeting his eyes, 'What you said earlier— about feeling guilty. You mustn't. What happened wasn't your fault. No one could have avoided that accident.'

She did look at him then because the silence was so long, burdened with tension, and when her green eyes locked with his narrowed grey gaze she turned her head quickly because what she had seen was compassion, pity. She couldn't handle that.

And he said huskily, 'You were so happy until then. I knew how badly you wanted that child. How could I not have felt the burden of guilt? It was like a ton weight.' He seated himself beside her and reached for her, tilting her small chin between the thumb and forefinger of one hand, forcing her to meet the shadowed power of his eyes. 'And I was right, wasn't I? It was something you couldn't spring back from. Your jealousy of Harry cut me like a knife. During that weekend I watched you freeze, die a little more inside. You can't imagine what it did to me. Culpability isn't easy to live with.'

Culpability. A draining word, defeating them, slicing through the tenuous bonds there had once been between them. Little wonder he had shut her out of his life, had sought out the warmth and vibrancy of the woman he had been unable to stop loving. And discovering she had borne him a son had only fuelled his obsession.

Compressing her lips, she twisted her head away and picked up her cutlery. Jealous of young Harry she had been, but only because the little charmer was his son. His and Zanna's. Not for the reasons he had manufactured in his head. She didn't know how he could be so blind, so insensitive to her feelings.

On the other hand, she knew very well, she thought drearily as she cut into her meat, suddenly and inexplicably ravenous. Even during their most intimate moments he had never pretended he loved her. And, because of that, she had never been able to confess how she felt. Protestations of love on her part would only have embarrassed him, made him feel trapped by the weight of it. And increased her own sense of vulnerability, which had been terrifying enough as it was.

And nothing she had said, it seemed, had lessened his unreasoning sense of guilt over the loss of their child. She didn't know how she could further help him over that hurdle, except by telling him that the consultant's dire prognosis had been unfounded, that she had, in fact, conceived again.

From the corner of her eye she saw him begin his own meal. He didn't seem to have much of an appetite. She sighed. She could help him to lose some of that sense of guilt, but she had no intention of doing so. Not yet. Perhaps not for a long time to come. Because for the first time in her life she was going to be utterly and completely selfish.

She was going to keep the fact of her pregnancy secret until she had sorted out a new life for herself and was better able to handle the future ramifications of the visiting rights, the watchful interest he would insist on taking in his child. It would be appalling to have to meet him at regular intervals. The only way she could kill off her futile, hopeless love for him was to cut him completely out of her life, never see him again. If he knew about the coming child he would make that impossible.

'The steak's good.' She had to say something, didn't she? Something, anything, to break the aching silence. Any moment now he would ask for her decision. And she would give it. And that would, irrevocably, end the marriage that had once been her whole existence.

But she wasn't going to think of that right now. Her metabolism was demanding sustenance and the meat was good, but needed something...

Her mouth watering, she reached for the marmalade she had unconsciously put out and unthinkingly spread it thickly over her steak, cut into it and popped a morsel into her mouth. Delicious.

And at her side Charles said tightly, 'You're pregnant.'

Beth swallowed convulsively, her face going scarlet. She felt as if she had been discovered doing something shameful. And unbidden, swift memory blazed across her mind.

Two months pregnant the last time. She and Charles dining out. Both choosing Châteaubriand. And then that sudden craving for, of all crazy things, marmalade on her meat...

The discreet lilt of the waiter's eyebrows had, to give him his due, been hardly discernible. But Charles had lounged back in his chair, and even now, in memory, she could see the indulgent curve of his mouth, the warm pride in his eyes as he'd drawled amusedly, 'My wife is in what is politely known as an interesting condition, and has developed a few outrageous eating habits.'

And she had glowed then, then and for the remainder of the evening, secure with him, so secure...

Her eyes winged up to his, her cheeks still stained with hectic colour, and she saw a blaze of something she could only translate as that one closely shared memory in those narrowed grey depths, and she couldn't for the life of her, even attempt to lie to him.

'You've always blushed easily,' he said with soft irony, his shadowed eyes dropping from her warm, shell-shocked face, down over her rounded, thrusting breasts to her narrow little waist. 'When were you going to tell me? Or weren't you?'

'I——' Oh, lordy, how could she answer that? 'When I'd got used to the idea myself,' she temporised after a frantic search through her scrambled brain.

But all he said, his voice dark, was, 'I wonder.' He gave her a tight cynical smile before he got to his feet, removing her glass of wine. 'In your condition, you don't drink,' he told her in a hard, accusatory tone. 'Eat. I'll make the coffee.'

Although he had left the greater part of his own meal, she saw the sense in what he had said. She had eaten nothing all day and mixing alcohol with pregnancy wasn't the best of ideas. But already he was taking over and she dragged her mind together and began using it furiously while she ate as much as she could, the food she had been so ravenous for now tasting like so much sawdust.

And she knew she had been right to concentrate on working things through when he carried their coffee-mugs through to the sitting-room, gestured her to the only comfortable chair the cottage boasted, and straddled the hearth.

'There is no question now of a divorce, a trial separation, whatever.' His eyes were harder than she'd ever seen them. 'No matter how little it seems to mean to you, you are my wife, and you are carrying my child. And you are coming home to South Park with me, tomorrow, where you will be watched over with merciless attention by the best consultant I can find. And if you have any irresponsible notions about bringing up our child on your own, forget them. I would apply for custody. Make no mistake about that. Do you understand?'

Perfectly. It was what she had expected, the reason she had kept her secret. There was no way he would let her go now. And yes, he would have no hesitation in applying for custody, and with his financial clout, his standing, her own seemingly flighty desertion of him, he might just win. In any case, she dared not take that risk.

Zanna had done another of her disappearing acts, taking Harry with her. And although he could demand access to his son, it could be tricky. But she, as his legal wife, would be allowed no such freedom. The coming child was his legitimate offspring. And what he had, he kept.

His reason for marrying her in the first place had hinged upon his desire for a family to inherit the newly affluent Savage dynasty, to enjoy the fruits of his hard labour, his clever brain, to carry on the line.

So she said, 'Yes, I understand you,' her voice emerging rustily as she mentally injected a dose of stiffening into her backbone. He might have her neatly trapped, but there was no way he was going to make her *feel* trapped, no more than by the bounds of her living space, anyway.

At one time she would have agreed to anything and everything he asked of her, because of the love she bore him. But not now. Not any more. She would wean herself away from the dependency of her love for him. And she said crisply, 'I agree to go back to South Park with you, to run your home as you expect me to, entertain your guests. But, in return, I have stipulations of my own to make.'

Uncrossing her slender legs, she got to her feet, moving restlessly over the tiny room to put her coffee-mug down on a table. The dark intensity of his unwavering regard was making her feel overwhelmed. And that, the disturbing sexual magnetism that was such an intrinsic part of his make-up as far as she was concerned, was something she was going to have to get to grips with, fight, emerge, if not exactly a winner, not a victim either.

'And those are?' His cool, almost indifferent tone made her shudder. She knew him well enough to recognise the concealed threat. Tilting her chin, she disregarded it, pacing the room with a swirl of soft skirts, aware of the way his guarded eyes followed every movement she made, yet desperately pretending she wasn't.

'I need to work. To achieve something in my own right. I need to be more than your appendage.' Needed something to hold on to, something to take her mind off the empty sham of their relationship. Something to blunt the pain of knowing that her old dream of teaching him to love her was completely hopeless.

'I see. And just how will that be achieved?'

'No hassle.' Stoically, she ignored the patronising tone. He had only ever seen her as someone who could be useful to him. Run his lovely home, entertain his weekend guests, bear him the sons and daughters he had decided he needed. He had never seen her as a woman who had needs that could not be satisfied by a gracious home to live in, beautiful clothes to wear, his attention in the bedroom when he felt so inclined.

Ignoring the knot of pain that had so annoyingly planted itself behind her breastbone, she continued coolly, 'Allie has often asked me to go back into partnership with her. We made a good team. And she wants to expand the area of the agency's activities. It's the sort of challenge I'd enjoy.'

Enough of a challenge to take her outside the closed and unsatisfactory arena of their marriage. True, she would have their child, and she would love him or her to distraction. But she would need something more, something outside the sterile boundaries of her marriage, if she were to keep her self-respect, her sanity.

'And the child?' He had finished his coffee and was pouring more of the wine for himself, the unspoken tension in him translating itself into the terse rattle of the neck of the bottle against the glass. 'If you are harbouring any delusions of putting on your business suit and prancing out to the office each day, leaving our child to the mercies of a hired nanny, then you can forget them.'

Which pulled her mouth into a straight line, made her eyes glitter like bright green glass, equalling the hardness she saw in his.

'I have no delusions,' she spat. None at all, not now. Not a single one was left to cloud the issue, which, she reminded herself, just in time, just before she lost her temper, was all to the good, wasn't it? 'I would be working purely in an administrative capacity and could do that from South Park. You worked from home often enough. Or used to,' she tacked on snidely, unwisely, she saw, recognising the slight upwards drift of one dark male brow. He wasn't a fool and would ferret out all her hang-ups if she didn't keep a more careful watch over her tongue.

Making herself relax because she was fighting for the chance to make a life for herself, distance herself from him and destroy the soul-draining, all-consuming love he so unconsciously called from her, she slowly walked to the chair she had vacated and resumed her seat, tilting her head in his direction, her expression so very carefully bland, tossing the ball straight back at him. 'Well? You agree?'

He gave her a coolly sardonic look then took a hard-looking pinewood chair from the chimney corner, swivelled it round and straddled it, resting his arms along the back, his wine glass held loosely

in one long-fingered hand. All this before he told
her with soft scorn, 'We seem to be reaching the
heart of the matter. You should have been honest
about this before. Am I so much of a tyrant?'

He lifted one wide, hard-boned shoulder in a
shrug so minimal as to make it practically non-
existent, the insouciant gesture clearly telling her
that whether she regarded him as a tyrant or not
was not of any particular interest to him. Then his
hard, incredibly sexy mouth curved into a smile that
held no humour at all as he stated, 'So you want
to fly. You were so greedy for some sort of freedom
outside our marriage that you used the grimy little
pretext of a trial separation in order to stretch your
wings. Our marriage, so it would seem, was not
enough of a challange.' He drained his glass, setting
it down carefully at his feet, turning the cold
scrutiny of his eyes back to her, his chilling assessment making her shake inside because she was
sure he could see beneath the calmness of the relaxed front she presented to the mass of miseries
deep inside.

Desperately, she bit back the scathing words of
bitter condemnation that crowded on her tongue.
How could she now explain that the conversation
which he knew she'd overheard between him and
Zanna had been the reason for the way she'd walked
out on their marriage?

How could she, when she had been so determined to get in there first, leading him to believe—
for the sake of her self-respect—that she had decided on a separation, pushing home that concept
because she hadn't been able to bear the final hu-

miliation of having him ask her to divorce him, leaving him free to marry the mother of his son?

She had spiked her own guns in that respect and she was damned if she was going to tell him the truth now. And he said, 'Your pregnancy, of course, has put an end to all that. However, within the boundaries of what you have outlined, I agree.'

Was she supposed to curtsy, or genuflect? she asked herself acidly, trying to make herself hate him because her next stipulation, his agreement so necessary, was going to be far harder to make.

It was growing darker now, the forest trees cutting out the last of the evening sunlight, casting a dark green shade that made the small room like an underwater cavern. Charles got to his feet, going to light one of the oil-lamps, and she said quickly, before her already shaky resolve could desert her, 'There is one last thing. I want us to have separate rooms. I don't want to sleep with you again.' She saw him go very still, the honed features having a demonic quality in the orange flare of lamplight.

The eyes he turned on her as he straightened were deep in their shadowed sockets, unreadable, his mouth thinned, accentuating its fascinating cruelty, but his voice was casual to the point of boredom as he thrust his hands into the pockets of his jeans and told her, 'You surprise me. Your response to my recent lovemaking has been, frankly, cataclysmic. Not to mention your avid initiation of the process on one or two quite memorable occasions earlier today. However, my dear, you can be assured that I would never waste my sexual energies on an unwilling woman.'

A furious scarlet stain covered her entire body at his calculatedly cold description of what had happened this morning, but she was shivering inside because she knew he would feel perfectly free to seek his sexual pleasures elsewhere. Preferably finding emotional and physical release with Zanna, who obviously still found him sexually exciting even if she balked at the constraints of marriage.

But it was a stipulation she had had to make. His lovemaking might be everything she craved, but for him it was meaningless, a mere assuaging of a natural appetite. And having him share her bed would only leave her feeling degraded, leaving her just as far away as ever from falling out of love with him, finding the self she had once lost in her unreasoning love for him and would be in danger of losing again.

'I'm tired.' Her small face was pale with the strain of knowing herself trapped by her own unthinking revelation of her pregnancy, of the sheer effort of determination that had led her to make the stipulations that would enable her to keep her self-respect.

She got to her feet, pushing the wings of dark hair away from her forehead, gesturing to the hideously unyielding sofa he had to have used last night. 'If you're not up to facing the rigours of that thing again, then I'm willing,' she said, making it clear that her insistence on separate sleeping arrangements was already in operation. And he lifted one straight black brow cynically.

'I'm flattered to hear that there's at least one area in our life where you're willing. I shall manage adequately; you take the bed.'

And then, before weak tears could betray her, she turned to the stairs, but his voice, cold and hard, stopped her, froze her in the ice of disgust.

'There is one thing, my dear wife—before we embark on the future of your choosing. I would like to be sure that the child you are carrying is mine, not Templeton's.'

CHAPTER NINE

FOR a moment Beth was too shocked and furious to move. Her heart beating like a drum, she felt a tide of angry colour flush over her face before it receded, leaving her feeling cold with a rage deeper than she had ever known before.

How dared he?

Hauling her shoulders back, scarcely knowing what she was doing, she marched rigidly back across the room, brought her hand up and cracked it across his hard mouth, using every last ounce of strength.

The harsh sound of the contact, emphasised by the silence of the room, gave her a small, momentary stab of satisfaction, but not enough to assuage the anger boiling inside her, not nearly enough.

Charles didn't even flinch and the brief flare of something that looked, oddly, like triumph died quickly and left his eyes like stone, betraying nothing. She might not have touched him, let alone slapped him with all the energy she possessed, and she raised her hand again, her already stinging palm ready to deliver one more blow, and then another— until she had worked the torment of her anger, her passionate disgust of what he had said, right out of her system.

But, without even seeming to move, he captured her wrist in one of his hands and held it between them, the dark red stain already spreading over his face in stark contrast with the pinched whiteness of the skin around his nostrils.

'A wife is allowed to slap her husband just once in her life. That option is no longer open to you. Try it again and I'll hit you back.' He released her hand then, stepping back as if he couldn't bear to be this close, and the grey of his gunfighter's eyes had turned to black and she knew he meant what he said.

Her own head came up, her green eyes defiant in the small pale oval of her face. And the clamour of her heartbeats pushed the breath from her lungs as she realised how she would almost have welcomed his physical violence, because it would at least be contact, of a kind, an indication that his emotions were involved, and that—anything— would be better than the cool scorn with which he now regarded her, the light sarcasm he had used to her when discussing the future of their marriage.

And that thought, more than anything else, made her draw back, lose the taste for confrontation. It was sick, and she disgusted herself. Physical violence had always been loathsome to her and, as far as she knew—and she knew him well—to him.

And then, with a cold sarcasm that made her shiver, and go on shivering, he told her, 'I take it that your reaction means you haven't slept with him. You'll have to forgive me for asking, but I did hear him propose marriage. And, being a cynic, I assumed you had given him the necessary encouragement.'

Beth turned away, all her mental and physical reserves brought into play in her effort to cross the room and walk up the stairs without breaking down completely. And, this achieved, by some large miracle, she lay awake for most of the night wondering how she was going to cope with the rest of her life.

'Oh, it is nice to be home!' Molly Garner heaved a sigh of pure pleasure, took her teacup and saucer from the low table and leaned back in her armchair, sipping contentedly. 'I don't care what country you're in, you can't get a decent cup of tea. Not that we didn't have a lovely time, of course, but——'

'It is nice to be home!' Beth supplied with a wide and wicked grin as she gathered her parents' holiday photographs together and stacked them neatly.

The windows were open and the distant sound of a lawn-mower was vaguely hypnotic in the somnolent late-summer afternoon and just outside the windows a bee buzzed drowsily in the voluptuous heart of a blowsy red rose.

For the first time in weeks Beth felt a layer of contentment close around her heart. And she said, meaning it more than her mother would ever know, 'It's nice to have you home. I've missed you both.'

In the few weeks she'd been back at South Park she had felt lonelier and emptier than she had ever done in her life. True, Allie had welcomed her suggestion of renewing their partnership with a whoop of delight and they'd been busy sorting out the legalities, future working procedure, and turning a little-used study which was tucked away behind the impressive library at South Park into an office for her use, complete with a computer link-up, filing cabinets and the like.

But nothing, not even starting back to work again, could ever make up for the cold sham of her marriage, and she shuddered involuntarily and her mother asked quickly, 'Cold, pet? Let me close that window.'

'I'm fine. Just a goose walking over my grave.' She found a smile for her spherical mother who was already struggling out of the depths of her chair, and went on smiling until her face felt stiff with the effort as Molly scoffed,

'It's nice of you to say it, but you wouldn't have had time to miss us, running around like that. France, wasn't it?'

Her parents hadn't been back home for five minutes before the gossips had gone to work. Nothing could be kept a secret in this close-knit community. So Beth had little option but to bend the truth.

'Near Boulogne. Charles was so often away at that time and Allie had a client she couldn't fix. It was only a short-term temporary thing, so I stepped into the breach. Charles managed to visit a couple of times.'

'Well, he must have done, mustn't he?' Mrs Garner responded drily. 'Otherwise I wouldn't be looking forward to a grandchild.'

Beth summoned a shaky smile but inside she was giving a sigh of relief. She was back now, keeping up appearances as Charles's wife, and if her mother ever got to know that she was doing so only because he had threatened to apply for custody of their child, with all the attendant publicity the court case would create, doubts cast upon her daughter's fitness for bringing up a child—no doubt with salacious tales of her sojourn in France with a man who had ended up proposing to her—she would be more than horrified.

She had been against the marriage in the first place. Not because Charles Savage was so far above the doctor's daughter both financially and socially—she wasn't that old-fashioned—but because of Zanna. Only a week before the wedding she had said worriedly,

'Have you really thought it out, pet? I don't want to spoil things for you, but I don't want to see you unhappy, either. Don't you think it's a little soon? He could be marrying you on the rebound, you know. Have you thought about that? No one could miss seeing the way he was with that Zanna Hall woman. She'll be a hard act to follow.'

But Beth hadn't thought about it, or only inasmuch as to convince herself that although he had made no pretence of being in love with her, spouted no pretty words, she, with her own deep and long-developing love for him, could teach him to need her as much as she needed him. It had been the supreme self-confidence of untried youth, the supreme folly. And, in the circumstances, the less her mother knew about the present situation, the better.

And now that lady was saying complacently, 'Your good news couldn't have been a better homecoming present. I'm going to have to buy lots of baby wool.'

Beth winced inside. Could her mother really have forgotten all those tiny jackets and caps, carefully

folded away in tissue paper, which she'd knitted
with such enthusiasm for the baby they'd lost?

No one ever mentioned the accident, and its tragic
aftermath. Everyone had been traumatised. They
seemed to think that if it wasn't mentioned it hadn't
really happened.

'And do tell...' Mrs Garner leaned forward to
pour them both another cup of tea. 'I heard that
Hall woman turned up at South Park—brazen as
ever, with her two-year-old son. Did you give her
short shrift? I know I would have done. That
woman has no sensibilities whatsoever! She's not
married, apparently.'

'I didn't see much of her,' Beth said, feigning
indifference. 'We had a houseful of guests for the
weekend and I was leaving for France almost immediately.' Any minute now her mother would be
relaying the news that young Harry bore a remarkable resemblance to Charles Savage, and Beth
didn't know quite how she was going to skirt round
that one. She could feel perspiration begin to break
out on her brow, in the palms of her hands but,
thankfully, her father walked in through the door.

'Any tea in the pot? I'm parched.' He flopped
down on the sofa next to Beth, running his hands
through his thinning grey hair. 'Soon be autumn,
and I can put the garden to bed. I know exercise
is good for me—drummed it into my patients often
enough, but——'

'But you'll spend the winter evenings reading
through the seed catalogues, mapping out new
borders, ordering plants, fretting to get out there
again,' his wife cut in drily, passing him a cup of
tea. 'Do you know, Beth, he paid Johnny Higgs a

small fortune to keep everything trim while we were away, and no sooner had he dumped the suitcases in the kitchen than he was out there, on his hands and knees with a magnifying glass looking for imaginary weeds, trimming hedges, mowing lawns...'

Amid the rueful laughter Beth got to her feet, smoothing down her skirts, making her excuses. 'Charles was away last night, but he said he'd be back by teatime. I must rush, if I'm to be there to meet him.'

They kept up the pretence, even in front of each other, treating each other politely, like strangers. He worked more from home now but every now and then had to go up to town, staying overnight to give himself two clear days at head office. And she always made sure she was around when she knew he was due, emerging from her office in time to tidy herself, ready to greet him with polite if stilted enquiries about the journey, offering him a drink to help him unwind, passing on snippets of local news she thought might interest him. No one would ever be able to accuse her of not keeping to their bargain.

'Well, don't rush too much,' her father advised gruffly as he walked with her to the door, an arm around her shoulder. 'Got to handle yourself with kid gloves from now on.'

It was the nearest either of her parents had got to mentioning her miscarriage, apart from the initial flood of shocked sympathy, and she wondered, belatedly, whether more openness would have helped during the long, distressingly miserable months that had followed.

Certainly, if Charles had been able to bring himself to explain that his deep feelings of guilt had been responsible for the distance he had put between them, then things would have been easier, and they would have grown closer instead of further and further apart. Especially if she had confided her own feelings of failure, the terrible feelings of inadequacy she'd gone through after she'd learned she might never conceive again.

But any closeness they might have achieved would have counted for nothing from the moment that Zanna and Harry put in an appearance, she reminded herself tartly as she settled herself behind the wheel of her car. The past was over and all the might-have-beens in the world would make no difference to the future.

Winding down the window and pasting a smile on her face, she waved to her hovering parents, calling brightly, 'Dinner with us tomorrow. Don't forget—seven o'clock sharp. And bring your holiday snaps; Charles won't want to miss seeing them.' And she drove away slowly because sudden, stupid tears were blurring her vision. She had a long way to go before she could calmly accept her life for what it was.

She entertained a great deal, worked hard for the agency, put on a bright face. And if her parents expressed concern over her pallor, the dark smudges beneath her eyes, she told them truthfully that she was being looked after by one of the leading obstetricians in the country—at Charles's instigation—and that he pronounced himself satisfied, said she was doing fine.

And when she and Charles were together, which happened as little as she could arrange it, she sometimes glanced up to find him watching her and, just for a moment, their eyes would hold. And there was something there she could not read, gave up even trying to, and pigeon-holed the enigmatic expression under the label of resentment.

He had to resent her presence, her nominal position as his wife. They both knew he had been willing to divorce her, to take the woman he loved as his wife, and they both knew that she, Beth, was only here because she was carrying his child, because the impossible-to-pin-down Zanna had walked out on him yet again.

His heart was with the flamboyant, vibrantly alive redhead; always had been, always would be. Every time he looked at her, Beth, he would resent her for not being Zanna.

She was a second-best wife, and knew it. But was learning to handle it, learning to make the most of her organising abilities and put them to good use in the build-up of the agency. Learning, slowly and painfully, to erect an impenetrable wall around her heart.

Christmas and the New Year festivities came and went and Beth congratulated herself on handling everything perfectly. The big house was decorated with branches of holly cut from around the estate, the huge open hearths alight with blazing logs, the hospitality lavish—right down to the silver bowls of Mrs Penny's aromatic punch.

Charles's brows had drawn together in a frowning black bar when he'd scanned the guest list he'd asked to see, but she'd ignored the obvious signs of his displeasure, knowing that he possessed enough self-control to be the perfect host, knowing that she had to fill the house with guests to be able to get through the season at all because she wasn't yet strong enough, self-contained enough, to be alone with him at this supposedly happy, family time.

But she was getting there, she assured herself, learning to live with his icy, slightly mocking politeness, learning to match it, learning not to care. And when he told her, 'There will be no more entertaining, apart from when your parents come for dinner, no more huge parties,' she simply dipped her head in cool submission and turned back to her work, feeding fresh data into the computer.

He had come to her office, which was unusual, and his interference in the way she ran the social side of their lives more unusual still. And the veneer of cool indifference was peeling along the edges of his voice as he bit out, 'You're running yourself ragged. If you don't give a damn about your own health, you should think about the child. From now on, you're going to do just that because, if you don't, I'll damn well make you.' And left the room, slamming the door behind him.

The child. Of course. The new life she was carrying inside her was his prime concern. The only reason she was here. But she couldn't feel resentful, couldn't wish the baby had never been conceived. It was all she had to live for now.

In all truth, she didn't regret Charles's strict veto. She was getting bulkier and slower, her body telling her it was time to be quiet. Entertaining so frequently, so lavishly, was, she recognised, becoming something of a strain.

But that didn't mean she could be content to spend much time alone with Charles. She knew, from the bitter expression she sometimes surprised in the depths of her eyes when she used her mirror, that she was on the verge of accepting her life as it was, the polished, surface-bright sham of her marriage.

However, alone with him, who could tell whether some remnant of emotion she hadn't quite managed to kill off might rear to shocking life and rend her with the pain of all that would-be forgotten love? She simply couldn't trust herself enough to run that risk.

Love didn't die to order; you couldn't switch it off because you had been hurt and humiliated.

But she was getting there.

So, as January drew to its storm-swept, bleak close she devised other methods of distancing herself.

Her mother was more than happy to agree to her suggestion of a week in London, buying new maternity clothes, but still she said, 'You won't want too many, surely? Only a couple of months to go and if you're anything like I was... after you were born, I couldn't wait to donate those dreadful tents to the vicar's jumble sale! Mind you, I felt guilty afterwards because they might have come in again. But, as it turned out, you were the only one—we did so want you to have a brother or sister. But, with any luck, you and Charles will have lots of babies—South Park needs filling, don't you think?'

Beth closed her eyes on the pain of that artless remark. The child she was carrying would be the only one. That her marriage to Charles was in name only, physical intimacies relegated to the past, was her bitter secret. South Park's empty rooms would remain so.

Nevertheless, her chin came resolutely up. As an only child herself she had never felt deprived or lonely. She'd always had lots of friends in the village and at school and she would make sure that her child had them too.

And of course the week away stretched to just over two. There were plenty of shows Beth suddenly found she had to see, exhibitions which would be a pity to miss.

'Pity not to pamper ourselves now we're here,' she told her mother when she pointed out that their week was up. 'It's nice to see all we want to see in a leisurely fashion. You're not fretting about Dad, are you?'

'No, of course not.' Molly Garner smiled up at the hotel waiter who had brought a rack of fresh toast to their breakfast table. 'He manages very well on his own. He probably enjoys the silence. He's always accusing me of talking too much! No, Beth, it's you I'm worried about. Is everything all right?'

'Of course!' she answered, too quickly, and made a great production of buttering toast she didn't want. Beneath the prattling inconsequentiality of her mother's conversation there was an astute mind. And she'd always been a little over-protective of her only offspring. She would do well to remember that. So she tacked on offhandedly, 'Whatever makes you ask?'

'You've changed. I can't quite put my finger on it. But there's a sadness in your eyes that sometimes makes me want to cry.'

'Idiot!' It was an effort to achieve a light tone, to force a smile. If her mother had remarked on a new hardness, she would have privately agreed with her and silently congratulated herself on the achievement of her aims. But sadness?

Did what she had gone through really show that much? Did her eyes say one thing even as her brain was saying another? Had she still such a long way to go in her determination to wrench all that ill-begotten love for her husband out of her heart? It didn't bear thinking about. So she smiled resolutely at her troubled parent and passed it off.

'You're imagining things. You're looking at a woman who has backache, frequent heartburn, puffy ankles and bruises to show where a certain little monster is playing football with its mother's insides! Now, what shall we do today? The exhibition of Victorian jewellery? Or shall we go back to Harrods to look at that suit I almost talked you into buying on Wednesday?'

But she couldn't stay away forever, and, certainly, Charles gave her no indication that he had missed her. But, then, why should he? They had stopped pretending when his feelings for Zanna had been brought out into the open.

Besides, she had plenty to occupy herself. She had the excuse of the agency work to catch up on and so was able to shut herself in her office each day, emerging to share a hasty and largely silent dinner with Charles, going immediately after to her room on the pretext of tiredness.

Not that it was a pretext, of course. She was tired, her body ached with it. But her mind wouldn't let her rest. And, one early March night, with the icy rain lashing her window panes, she gave up all attempt to capture elusive sleep, pulled a wrap over her increasing girth and waddled as quietly as she could to the nursery.

Although Charles had said nothing—one raised brow had been enough to tell her he thought her crazy but was willing to pander to the whims of the pregnant—she had insisted on having the room redone.

It was here that Harry had slept—not that she blamed the little innocent, but she couldn't forget how she had seen his parents hovering over him as he lay in the cot that had been bought with such excitement for the baby she had lost.

And even now, if she allowed the forbidden memory over the wall she had built in her mind, she could see Zanna in that clinging satin nightdress, Charles holding her, hear again those fervent words of welcome for the child she had brought him...

Wandering around, touching things, she felt herself begin to relax and sat down on the edge of the single bed she had had one of the gardeners bring into the room. She would sleep here for the first few months of the baby's life as she had every intention of feeding it herself and no intention whatsoever of asking Charles to vacate the adjoining master suite.

The thought of him, now, lying sprawled in the huge double bed, did nothing to help her determination to relax so she thrust it unceremoniously away and hauled herself back to her feet.

Mrs Penny had insisted on carrying up the packages of baby clothes she'd spent an extravagant small fortune on in London, saying, with some justification, that there was enough stuff here already to clothe an army of infants before pushing the new consignment on to the top of the series of open shelves that ran down one side of the cream-painted nursery cupboards.

They had been there for weeks now and needed sorting, placing on the right shelves, and, even standing on tiptoe, Beth couldn't quite reach. Not willing to give up the attempt, she caught hold of the low nursing chair and dragged it across the floor. Clambering up on it, she could just reach, her fingers closing around the piles of tiny, tissue-wrapped garments, the boxed baby toys she hadn't been able to resist.

And the first intimation she had that she was not alone was the rough sound of a crude oath and the strength and warmth and power of the male arms circling her body.

'Just what the hell do you think you're doing?' His voice cracked like the lash of a whip and her whole body went on fire as his arms tightened, swinging her gently down from the chair and setting her on the ground. He was still holding her, but loosely, and she twisted round within the circle of his arms and then wished she hadn't.

He was wearing one of his short towelling robes, hastily tied, and she knew from experience he would be naked beneath it. He never wore anything between the sheets. And just looking at him, at the

severely carved angles and planes of his unforget-
table features, the dusting of crisp body hair that
coarsened the olive-toned skin of his exposed chest
and long, firmly muscled legs, her heart began to
thunder and her thought processes lay down and
died.

'Well?' he demanded, his eyes flaying hers,
making her lower her thick lashes very quickly to
deny him the knowledge of the effect he could still
have on her.

Pushing her tongue over her dry lips, she
managed, 'I still haven't sorted out the baby things
I bought in London.' She had to stay calm, she had
to. Now wasn't the time to throw a wobbly. But
after months of conducting limited conversations
in tones of lightly veiled sarcasm or, what was
probably worse, with polite boredom, his sudden
anger, that show of real emotion, had her running
scared, unsure of how to handle it.

It didn't fit into her undeviating delineation of
what their type of marriage should be, and without
her carefully drawn-up guidelines to cling on to she
was in danger of drifting woefully off course.

'So you decided, after weeks, to do it right now.
Couldn't it have waited until you could have asked
someone else to reach the stuff down?'

He had released her now, stuffing his hands into
the pockets of his robe, rocking back a little on the
heels of his bare feet. And she stepped back, away
from his overpowering sexual appeal, knocking
against the back of the chair and earning herself
an impatient scowl.

'I couldn't sleep.' Did she have to sound so over-
wrought? she asked herself edgily. And why was

she so suddenly aware of how truly awful she looked, her bulky, clumsy body forcing her to stand with her feet planted wide apart, the weight she had put on extending to her face, giving her the beginnings of a double chin?

'Neither could I,' he admitted, his rarely seen smile flickering briefly along his beautiful male mouth. 'That's why I heard you blundering about in here.'

Blundering. She bit down on her lip at his choice of word. He might as well come right out with it and tell her she looked and moved like a whale out of water.

She swung quickly away, furious with herself. Why did it matter? Women in her condition shouldn't care if they were unattractive, and minding that he should describe her as blundering was surely abnormal, especially since he had never really wanted her at all, but had simply used her because she was his wife and was available.

But his cool fingers caught her hand, trapping it beneath the tensile strength of muscle and bone, and the intonation of gentleness in his voice was something she hadn't heard since she had run out on him to go to France.

'As neither of us can sleep, why don't we do the job together?' His hands went to her shoulders, exerting a soft yet firm pressure as he sat her down in the nursing chair then turned in one fluid movement to reach the pile of packages and carriers from the top shelf. 'You unwrap them and tell me where to put them.'

The old, almost forgotten warmth and tenderness was right back in his voice, in the dark grey

eyes that slanted an understanding smile towards
her, and she sat there, feeling like a beached sea
mammal, wondering at the ease with which he
breached her carefully erected wall.

But only a small breach, surely, she informed
herself, the merest trickle of all that she shouldn't
allow getting through her defences. So she said, to
put the matter right, 'There's really no need for
you to bother,' her voice carrying just the right
amount of disparagement, not enough to sound
offensive.

He gave her a quick underbrow look, sucked in
his breath, then responded lightly, 'No bother. I'd
like to get acquainted with my heir's wardrobe.'

That figured, she thought, attempting to stir an
inner resentment that simply wasn't there to stir,
so she gave up trying and the coil of tension inside
her was slowly released, and she went with it, letting
her guard down because her brain had gone on
hold, she recognised, not really caring much at all.

And she actually found herself enjoying un-
wrapping the tiny garments, running her fingers
over the soft wool, the tiny silken ribbons, gurgling
with laughter as he held a minute bootee between
his long fingers, his expression wholly perplexed
male.

'You wouldn't think anything could be small
enough to fit into this.'

'You could be right.' Tomorrow she would regret
the lowering of her defences, but right now she was
simply allowing herself to relax, to enjoy the
closeness that had been growing over the last half
an hour. 'The way he kicks, he could emerge
wearing soccer boots—size twelve,' she said then

winced as a hefty movement served to prove her point.

'What is it, Beth?' With a swiftness that took her breath away, Charles was on his knees beside her, his brow darkly furrowed as he took her hands in his. 'Are you in pain?'

The amazing thing was, he looked as if he cared, Beth thought on a dizzying wave of stunned disbelief. In the space of half an hour he had reverted to being the warm, caring man who had been her much loved husband before that accident, before Zanna's return. It made her nervous; she didn't know how to handle it. She had been so sure she was at last schooling all that hopeless love for him out of her heart, and yet...

'No.' She shook her head, the soft wings of her hair flying around her flushed face. 'He's decided to go in for disco dancing, I think.'

Relief washed his anxious features but his eyes held a hesitancy that was completely new in her experience of him as he asked huskily, 'I'd like to feel our child move. Would you mind?'

In her experience of him, he had always taken what he wanted, and right now she was seeing a side of him she hadn't known existed. And, gently, she took his hand and laid it over the bulge of her stomach and the look of incredulous wonder in his dark eyes as Junior obliged with a well aimed kick brought tears to her eyes.

Still kneeling, he moved closer, an arm around her, his hand still resting gently, reassuringly, over her stomach, and for long, timeless moments his eyes held hers, her stupid heart leaping and jumping like a wild thing as he told her quietly, 'You are beautiful, Beth. Never more so, in my eyes, than you are right now.' And then the moment was gone as he grinned, his brows rising. 'There he goes again! No wonder you can't sleep if he keeps this up all night!' Lifting his hand, he tilted her chin between his thumb and forefinger, holding her eyes with his. 'Tell me something—we keep referring to the baby as "he". Will you be disappointed if we have a daughter?'

She shook her head, half dazedly, scarcely comprehending. This was the type of intimacy she had written out of their marriage—for the sake of her self-respect, her sanity. And here she was, lapping it up, weak fool that she was. Her condition must be making her especially vulnerable. But she managed huskily, 'No. Will you?'

'Of course not.'

And, silently, she echoed his words in her head. Of course not. He already had a son. He would feel no driving desire to sire a male child to rear in his image. But, strangely, even that thought had no power to wound and she dismissed it, every cell in her body melting as he stood up, pulling her with him, a muscle working at the side of his jaw as he told her, his voice thick with something nameless, something that made her bones go weak, 'I want to sleep with you tonight. Just to hold you in my arms, you and our child, nothing else.'

Beth couldn't speak for the emotion clogging her throat, and his wide, sexy mouth firmed with determination as he swept her up in his arms, telling her, 'The world went black for me when I saw you teetering around on that chair. Tonight I need the reassurance of holding you close, keeping you safe.'

And as if he would listen to no argument, no protest, he carried her through the partly open door into the master suite and gently laid her on the huge double bed, tucking the soft duvet carefully around her.

Beth blinked back tears, snuggling into the warmth, her face burrowing into the soft down pillow, breathing in the faint, slightly spicy scent of the aftershave he used, the heady, musky male presence of him.

It had been a year since she had shared this room with him, this bed. It felt like coming home and fresh tears glittered in her eyes because he had never, ever admitted a need for reassurance before.

Finding her tottering around on that nursery chair, reaching for packages, had brought back bad memories of the accident that had caused her miscarriage, brought back the feelings of guilt he had no right to have. And when she felt the mattress dip beside her, his arms reach out for her, she knew why she had made no protest and snuggled herself into the protective curve of his body, promising herself that they both needed this one night out of time.

Tomorrow, she thought, as his deep and regular breathing told her that he had drifted immediately off to sleep, things would be back to where they were, because, knowing what they both knew, how could they be different?

CHAPTER TEN

BETH came awake quickly. She knew she was alone in the big double bed. She hadn't slept so deeply, so peacefully in months and she levered herself up, stacking the pillows behind her and leaning back.

A smile spread unstoppably over her features and she chewed on her lower lip to prevent it getting out of hand. Slowly, she admonished herself. Take it slowly.

But her thoughts were running around like mice, rushing onwards as if she'd pushed the fast-forward button in her brain. They wouldn't be stopped, so she let it all happen, all the tenuous hopes and needs coalescing into one great big beautiful whole.

Last night Charles had demonstrated that he was still capable of caring for her. Even if she wasn't Zanna, she was his wife, the soon-to-be mother of his child. And they had taken comfort and re-assurance from each other, despite her stipulation that theirs should be a marriage in name only, despite the way their lives had been compartmentalised, never touching each other.

But it needn't go back to being that way, need it?

Daylight was struggling to get through the thickness of the lined velvet curtains but Beth was going to stay right where she was until she had everything sorted out in her mind.

She would have to have a long and serious talk with him, because maybe she'd been wrong to try to immure herself behind the wall of her own painstaking construction. If they could speak openly about his feelings for Zanna then maybe they could reach a better understanding.

Perhaps the wayward redhead's second desertion of him had killed his obsession? She could only hope and pray it had. Because if it had, and she was able to stop living on the knife-edge of wondering just when the other woman would walk back into his life, and take him away, then she needn't tell herself that her love for him was self-defeating, masochistic. She would have no need to try to kill it.

She had been afraid to question him before. He had known she knew the truth about Harry and Zanna, his desire to be with them, and digging down into it all would only have heaped more pain and humiliation on her head, and she hadn't been brave enough, strong enough to face that.

But the way he had been with her last night, so gentle, admitting his own vulnerability, his need for her comfort and reassurance, had given her an injection of courage, and, somehow, she had found more of the same inside herself. Enough courage to ask him to talk this whole thing through.

An extremely perfunctory tap on the door heralded Mrs Penny's arrival with a breakfast tray, and, her thoughts disrupted, Beth beamed and called out a bright good morning.

She was actually feeling more hopeful now than she had ever done, even during the first months of their marriage when she'd been sure she could make him love her. Now, though, she wasn't asking for the moon, the sun and the stars. Just to reach a new understanding, a hope that they could build on the foundations of their marriage and, eventually, create something of enduring strength. So the moon alone would do for starters!

'Breakfast in bed, and you're to stay right where you are until noon. Charlie-boy's orders.' The housekeeper put the tray on her knees and rushed around pulling back the curtains. 'He's gone to the bank and he said to tell you he'll be back before lunch and you're to take it easy until then. And about time, too, if you ask me.'

'I'm not,' Beth responded wryly. 'Not that it matters. You'll tell me, anyway.'

'Too right. Eat your eggs.' Mrs Penny shot her a huffy look which was quite at variance with the gleam in her eyes. 'And while we're at it, I'm happy to see you back where you belong. I don't hold with married folks having separate rooms.' She planted her hands on her hips. 'It may be considered sophisticated and civilised in some circles but I call it plain unnatural! And mind you drink your orange juice.'

There wasn't much that escaped Mrs Penny's gimlet eye, Beth thought as she dutifully consumed scrambled eggs and toast. She would have tied her disappearance and her subsequent strained relationship with Charles up with Zanna's arrival, back in June.

And she'd made no attempt to hide her disapproval when she'd remarked on the unmissable likeness between Harry and his father. She'd been at South Park so long that she regarded herself as one of the family and wasn't afraid to speak her mind...

Beth put the tray to one side and slid out of bed. Looking over her shoulder, back into the past, wasn't going to help her attempts to build a new future with Charles. They needed to talk; she had to tell him that if she could be sure his obsession with Zanna was a thing of the past, with no danger of any future resurrection, then she was willing to forget everything that had happened and try to make their marriage something of value for both of them.

She had tried so hard to stop loving him, and had believed she had succeeded. But one show of tenderness from him, a night spent held so gently in his arms, had shown her how wrong she had been. She could no more stop loving him than stop breathing.

As if to reinforce her mood of hopefulness the weather had changed, producing a day that was the perfect harbinger of spring. Unable to settle to work or to take the rest Charles had prescribed, Beth slipped a coat over one of the light wool maternity dresses she'd bought in London and had not got round to wearing yet, and slipped outside.

The wind was chilly but light enough to be disregarded and the sun was shining, the sky an aching, beautiful blue, dotted with small, fluffy white clouds. It would be another month before the buds on the trees began to swell and unfurl their leaves, but there were already drifts of small wild daffodils spreading their gleam of golden promise beneath them.

Deciding to pick a few of the blooms and make an arrangement for the dining-room table—which, she acknowledged wryly, would help pass the time before Charles returned and they could have that talk, the thought of which was producing butterflies of nervous excitement inside her—she set off across the wide gravelled drive, only to leap for the safety of the grass verge as a small scarlet sports car howled round the bend.

Her bulk made leaping for safety both undignified and difficult, and she scrabbled up from her hands and knees, her face scarlet with outrage and humiliation as she brushed the clinging particles of damp grass and soil from her hands and coat, turning annoyed green eyes to the car which had jerked to a gravel-spattering halt just past her and was now reversing at a ridiculous speed.

Through the side-window of the low-slung sports car Beth could see an expensive piece of luggage on the passenger-seat, a glimpse of long, silk-clad legs, the soft emerald-green fabric of a suit skirt riding high on lush thighs. And she knew, she just knew, and she could only stare woodenly as the other woman slid quickly out from behind the wheel and tossed out over the low roof of the vehicle,

'I broke all speed records getting from Heathrow only to run you down on your own driveway! Mind you, your size makes you almost impossible to miss—I never did get that big carrying Harry!'

Disparaging, heavily made-up eyes swept over Beth, taking in the grass stains on the front of her coat. 'You didn't hurt yourself, did you?'

Beth shook her head impatiently, ignoring the sudden pain in her side. Her heart was hurting too

much to let a little thing like stitch bother her.
Zanna was here again—the thing she had dreaded
had actually happened.

As lovely as ever, as vibrantly alive and charis-
matic as always—would Charles be able to resist
her?

She closed her eyes briefly as Zanna began to
walk around the back of the car and when she
opened them again she was standing directly in front
of her, running long, scarlet-tipped fingers through
the tumbling riot of her red-gold hair.

There was no sign of Harry. Beth wasn't going
to ask where the little boy was. And all she could
say, thinly, was, 'Heathrow? You flew over from
France?' Surely Charles didn't know about this.
Surely he didn't? He would be as dismayed and annoyed as she was herself—of course he would, she
told herself forcefully.

'Spain, actually. We've been in Spain for the last
few months.' Zanna twisted round, inspecting the
seams of her stockings, twitching at the pencil-slim
skirt of the obviously designer-made suit she was
wearing. And Beth wondered if she'd left the little
boy behind, in the care of some Spanish child-
minder while she obeyed the waywardly irresponsible impulse to fly over and see Charles again,
boost her already over-inflated ego by proving, yet
again, that he was hers for the asking...

But he wasn't! she screamed silently inside her
head. He'd been obsessed by Zanna—everyone
knew that—willing, at one time, to throw out his
wife for her sake. But he was too strong-minded,
too sensible, to allow himself to be put through that
kind of hell all over again. Of course he was!

So when Zanna gave a theatrical shudder and said, 'I'm too exotic for the English climate; hop in, I'll give you a lift back to the house,' Beth was able to give her a cold, hard stare and refuse.

'I'd rather walk. Why are you here?' As if she couldn't guess, she scorned, her soft mouth twisting, and Zanna returned her glare, her lovely head tipped on one side as she came right back.

'God, but you're a frigid bitch. No wonder Charles—anyway...' She shrugged, obviously thinking better of whatever it was she had been going to say, which, Beth reflected bitterly, didn't need spelling out, did it? 'Look at me as if I'm poison if you want to—just as you did back in June—you'll find out why I'm here soon enough.' She turned to flounce back to the car but stopped as the Range Rover Charles was driving braked to a halt as he rounded the bend.

'Charles—darling!' Zanna, her arms outstretched, ran towards the parked vehicle and Beth went icy cold, clutching her coat collar tightly around her throat, the race of her heartbeats threatening to choke her. Everything hinged on his reaction, the way he greeted the woman who had twice walked out of his life, leaving him devastated.

She saw him leave the car, heard the slam of the door as he closed it behind him, saw the brief interrogatory glance he shafted in her direction, the slight shrug of those impressively broad shoulders, covered in impeccable tweed, and then his austere features were irradiated by a smile of sheer pleasure as he held out his own arms and caught the flying, green-suited figure, pulling her into the hard curve of his body.

Jealousy knifed wickedly through Beth's veins. She couldn't stand here on the sidelines, overlooked, one moment longer. She couldn't watch, but she couldn't help hearing Zanna's shriek of delight, her breathless, 'Darling—I've come back! Isn't it wonderful? Kiss me, do!'

It was unbelievable, incredible, and yet it was happening all over again. Zanna only had to put in an appearance to have the so adult, so controlled Charles Savage acting like a besotted schoolboy. Beth couldn't cope with it and, fighting back a tide of nausea, forced her trembling legs to carry her back to the house.

The moment—the very moment—she got him on his own she would give him a huge chunk of her mind! And then walk out. No court in the land would give custody to a man who could behave as he did!

Reaching the hall, she closed the main door behind her and ground her small teeth together in temper. Anger was the only way to stop herself bursting into broken-hearted tears. All her foolish hopes for the future had been ground into the dust because Zanna Hall had chosen to flick an eyelash in his direction!

So much for last night's gentle interlude. The other woman only had to give him that gorgeous smile and he conveniently forgot everything else— his wife, his responsibilities, his marriage vows!

Stamping towards the stairs, she made it halfway up before she bent double, gasping in pain. And below her, Mrs Penny, with an armful of freshly ironed sheets, called anxiously,

'What is it? Are you all right?'

'Oh, fine,' Beth answered, catching her breath. She sat down on the stairs. 'I think the baby's on its way.'

'Not to panic.' Mrs Penny put the bundle of sheets on a side-table. 'Better early than overdue. Where's that husband of yours?'

'I haven't the least idea.' The outright lie was better than having to admit that he was still devouring the love of his life in the middle of the drive! She was through with him. Through! Rage was the only salvation she could look for.

'Typical,' Mrs Penny muttered, hurrying up the stairs towards her. 'When you need them they're missing. When you don't they're crawling all over you, getting underfoot. Come on.' A helping arm heaved Beth to her feet. 'Phone your dad, he'll get you to the hospital. And I'll pop up and fetch your bag. Not to worry.'

Giving birth was the least of her worries, Beth thought sourly as she picked up the phone while the housekeeper rushed upstairs to fetch the bag Beth had packed a week ago. She would rather her father drove her. She didn't want Charles anywhere near her because she would only bawl him out, rip him to shreds with her tongue. And that wouldn't do her blood-pressure much good.

She began to punch numbers but hadn't got beyond the first two when a second contraction, much stronger than the first, had her dropping everything in sheer amazement.

And, of course, it was Charles who drove her. He had walked into the hall, one arm casually draped around Zanna's shoulders, and had sized up the situation immediately.

Putting the dangling receiver back on its rest, he'd taken the bag from the panting Mrs Penny and ushered her out of the door, lifting her into the passenger-seat of the Range Rover, which was parked at the front, right beside Zanna's showy sports job.

'You can drive me, because it will be quicker,' Beth told him, tight-lipped, as he swung in beside her, firing the ignition. 'But after that I don't want you near me.' She wiped the beads of perspiration from her upper lip with the back of her hand, meeting his narrowed, sideways glare defiantly. 'I wouldn't want the responsibility of keeping you from your little playmate. I'm sure she's got lots of lovely games for you to enjoy while I'm out of the way!'

'And what the hell is that supposed to mean?' His hands were tight on the wheel as they shot out of the main gates and on to the narrow country road, and his voice was a threat. But Beth had other things to think of right now and she tossed back exasperatedly,

'You know what it means! I overheard you talking, remember?' She winced, holding on to the edges of her seat as they flew over a hump-backed bridge. Perspiration dewed her small pale face all over again, but it had nothing to do with the speed. He was driving fast, but it was a controlled speed. He knew these roads like the back of his hand and wasn't taking any risks. And when she'd regained her breath she castigated, 'When she brought your son to meet you, back in June, you'd have divorced me like a shot to marry her. I only agreed to come back to you because I was pregnant——'

Again the spiking, clawing pain, but she howled straight through it. 'She walked out on you again, didn't she? Oh, I know she told you she was tired of being a single parent, and Harry needed his father, but she still walked out in the end. And I hoped you'd think twice about letting her do that to you again. But no, oh, no!' Her even, white teeth showed in a mirthless smile. 'The minute she shows again you're all over her like a rash—holding her, kissing her. You make me sick!'

He shot her a dark, complicated look. There were so many different emotions colouring his eyes black, too many to untangle, and she wasn't interested in trying, was she? she questioned herself snappily as he turned his attention back to the road and told her heatedly, 'You've got more than a few wires crossed.'

'Is that so?' Cool indifference might be more telling than any amount of justifiable ire and she turned her head to look out of the window at her side.

They had left the village behind and were on the main road and it wouldn't take longer than another five minutes to reach the exclusive private maternity home where she was booked in. She couldn't wait—in more ways than one!

'Beth——'

'Don't try to soft-soap me!' she grated through whatever it was he was beginning to say. 'And don't think I can't see through you. If you want to keep your options open, fine. But don't look to me. Whether Zanna stays or goes, it's all one to me because I won't be coming back. Not this time.'

For some crazy reason her throat clogged, unshed tears stinging at the backs of her eyes. She blinked furiously, aware of his hard sideways stare, the harsh intake of his breath.

And just for a moment his foot eased on the accelerator, as if he was contemplating pulling out of the traffic on to the side of the road, the better to give his full attention to the row they were having. But as a fresh spasm gripped her she gave a shuddering gasp and closed her eyes and his foot went down again. And all he said was, with a kind of bitter calm, 'We'll talk this over in a day or two. Right now I suggest you save your energy. You're hysterical.'

He could be right, Beth anguished, her eyes glued shut. Finally bringing things out into the open, speaking her mind, showing her utter disgust at the way things were between him and Zanna, had helped to take her mind off the horrible thought of having her baby in a lay-by. And now, in the tense silence, she wasn't so sure she was going to be able to avoid such an undignified happening!

In the event, it was the early hours of the following morning before the tiny, red-faced bundle was laid in her arms. Beth's heart went out instinctively, irredeemably and eternally and as her fingers stroked gently over the velvety cheek she whispered, 'Your name is Aidan John, my precious.'

'No "Charles"?' Soft-footed, Charles stood in the open doorway, the look in his eyes unrevealing. He advanced very slowly. 'Let's see—Aidan, because you like the name, I presume. John, for your father. But nothing for me, his father?'

Although she had told him she didn't want him near her, he had insisted on staying and, if she was honest, she had been more than merely grateful for the way he'd offered his hand for her to mangle, the way he'd stroked something cool and slightly fragrant over her heated skin. He'd never been more than inches away, completely supportive, and now, although she made a half-hearted attempt to come up with a withering comment, she couldn't find one.

She was tired but completely euphoric and now, with her hour-old son in her arms, wasn't the time to start another unholy row. But her unresisting capitulation, the tenderness in her smile as she glanced from her tiny son to his father, surprised her, and she acknowledged huskily, 'Charles Aidan John Savage—to be known as Aidan to avoid confusion.'

'Ah. Of course.' He had reached the bedside and was hunkering down, unfurling his son's tiny fingers, and devils were dancing in his sexy eyes as he murmured, 'I think it's time you got some rest, Mrs Savage. I'm glad to see you've worked your way through your own particular confusion.'

As if on cue, one of the nurses came in, took the sleeping baby and dimmed the light.

'Rest now, Mrs Savage,' she echoed, 'and if there's anything you need, just press the bell. Mr Savage . . . ?' The tilt of a blonde eyebrow was frankly flirtatious, the blue eyes full of female assessment, and Beth felt a sleepy smile drift across her mouth. Maybe she should feel jealous, but she didn't. Women had been giving Charles Savage the come-and-get-me since he'd reached his late teens and there was no room for jealousy or resentment, just a glorious sense of pride. Which was strange, she pondered exhaustedly as she heard him reply,

'Is staying put until his wife falls asleep,' and felt the rough, needing-a-shave brush of his cheek against hers as the dark waves of sleep pulled her under and her last conscious thought was that maybe he was right. Maybe her confusion was over.

In the early afternoon, holding court among a positive bower of hot-house flowers—the largest and most lavish of which had come from Charles— Beth knew that nothing was over, certainly not her 'confusion', if that was what he'd thought her decision to remove herself from his life to be.

He had phoned much earlier, full of supposedly loving enquiries, but she'd cut him short, saying her room was full of gabbling visitors, which was true—except for the gabbling bit—and that she couldn't hear herself think—which wasn't true at all because she'd heard the hard bite in his voice when he'd said he'd be with her later.

And now her parents were on their way out, taking Mrs Penny with them because she'd begged a lift to see the new arrival. And Allie inched her way in as they were going out, and although Beth would have welcomed the opportunity to have a good long thinking session, planning exactly what she would say to Charles when he got his two-timing, louse-like person here, she greeted her best and oldest friend with pleasure.

After the obligatory peek into the cradle, and enthusiastic cooings, Allie laid her offering of spring flowers on the counterpane and grimaced.

'Coals to Newcastle, I see! Never mind, I've got something you might appreciate more.' She put a bulky package on Beth's knees. 'It came to the agency this morning. There was a covering letter so I know what it is. Go on, open it!'

It was, it transpired, after she had dealt with Sellotape and brown paper, bound proofs of William's latest book, the one she had worked on with him. And her face went pink with embarrassment as she read the accompanying card:

If you ever need your job back, or anything else, don't hesitate. I'll always be here. Yours, Will.

Which was misguided of him, but sweet, and not at all helpful when a narrow-eyed Charles walked into the room and enquired, so silky-smooth, 'Someone sent you a book? Hi, Allie.' He glanced in the other girl's direction, but only briefly; he was intently reading the message on the piece of pasteboard he'd taken from Beth's nerveless fingers.

And then his eyes went black as outer space as he tossed the card back on the bed and took the two strides necessary to have him hovering over the cradle.

Beth knew, she just knew what was going on in his twisted, devious mind and a wildness took over her brain as she hissed, regardless of Allie's presence, 'If you're looking to see if there's any likeness—forget it. And if you mention tests to establish paternity, I'll kill you!'

He slewed round on his heels, his face granite, the impeccable cut of the dark suit he was wearing making him seem unapproachable, the menace in him distancing him from his surroundings as he clipped out coldly, 'Save your breath. Your reaction to my accusation, back in France, convinced me. You wouldn't have put a foot back over my doorstep if I'd had the slightest doubt.'

'I'll—I'll be off, then.' Allie's fluttery, awkward words were lost to them both as Beth sniped back at him.

'You do have a nice trusting nature, don't you?' she said, and didn't even flinch when his brows came down in a threatening bar.

'So it seems. I'd appreciate it, though, if you could acquire one, too.'

His effrontery took her breath away and she opened her mouth on a howl of protest. But he covered her lips with a none-too-gentle hand and warned her darkly, 'Don't utter another sound until I've had my say.' Leaving her propped amid the pillows, her lips compressed but her chin at a defiant angle, he put the 'Do Not Disturb' sign on the outside of the door, tossed Allie's flowers and William's bound proofs on to the floor, and lay on the bed, his arms folded behind his head, ignoring her snort of outrage.

'I've been trying to figure your behaviour out ever since you came up with the stupid idea of a trial separation.'

'It was one of the most sensible things I'd ever done.' He might have commanded her to keep quiet, but he couldn't make her keep her mouth shut. And she wished he'd get off the bed. He was far too close. So she tacked on viperishly, 'You hadn't come near me in months. I could have been a lodger, an octogenarian one at that, for all the interest you showed in me.' She gave him a fulminating sideways glare then stared sniffily at the ceiling, her arms folded beneath her breasts. She hadn't finished with him yet—she had barely begun!

'I've explained why.' For the first time, there was a trace of weariness in his voice and Beth's heart twisted sickeningly as he went on, 'If you knew how guilty I felt, you wouldn't have needed to ask why.'

No matter what he was; never mind if he would always put Zanna first, she had to acknowledge that he had been sincere about that. There had been no mistaking the pain in his voice when he had told her how he had blamed himself during those dreadful months after the accident. Her taunt had been unnecessary and out of order, and, to make up, she said diffidently, 'How could I have known, if you didn't tell me? And if it helps at all, I felt the guilt, too. You'd married me to have children— primarily, at least. I felt I'd let you down. Knowing I was unlikely to conceive again made me feel a failure, inadequate.'

He twisted suddenly on the bed, forcing her to look at him.

'You should have told me. Correction.' His hard mouth indented wryly. 'We should have told each other. Talked it through.' His eyes softened; his mouth did, too, as he brushed his lips over the suddenly sensitised skin of the shoulder her sleeveless nightgown left bare.

Beth shuddered helplessly. This confrontation wasn't going as she'd planned—she felt as if she'd been left in a mire of non-communication. If only they'd talked, not kept their guilt locked away inside themselves.

But that was all in the past, and they couldn't go back there, and he made that patently clear when he hoisted himself up on one elbow, his inescapable eyes on a level with hers as he informed her with studied patience, 'As I've been trying to explain, working out the motives for your behaviour has been beyond me. Until, that is, you came out with that hysterical spiel on the way here.'

'Hysterical?' she bridled, stung. 'It had nothing to do with what I was saying. You'd have been hysterical, too, if you'd thought you wouldn't make it in time to give birth in the proper place!'

'Rather more than that, I'd say. I would have been having a few rather serious doubts about my role in life.'

Unwillingly, her lips twitched. And then she remembered that jettisoning a husband was utterly serious. And, strangely, frightening, too. She sighed, very sober now, cold inside and, despite the peacefully sleeping baby, very alone. And Charles told her, 'It was only when you gabbled some nonsense about Harry being my son that I was able to put the facts together. Tell me, what exactly did you overhear, back in June?'

Nonsense? Beth's heart leapt then settled down to a sombre, heavy beat. She had heard what she had heard, and there was no way he could get round that. And, surely, he wouldn't want to, would he?

She ran the tip of her tongue over her dry lips, and husked out accusingly, 'She called you darling.'

'Is that all? She calls everyone darling.' He turned on his back again and closed his eyes, as if totally bored. Beth dug him sharply in the ribs.

'No, not all—not by a long chalk, and you know it.'

A small mew, followed by a hiccuping screech, had Beth scrambling down from the bed, lifting the tiny, protesting scrap of humanity from the cradle and scrambling back, Charles Aidan John tucked comfortably at her breast. And Charles muttered, 'Well, go on, then. Tell me.'

'I don't think this is the time or the place to be discussing the breakdown of our marriage,' Beth replied repressively. She would not let herself be upset. Not now. Later, perhaps. Or tomorrow. But now now.

Charles shifted round again, his eyes on the greedily suckling infant, his gaze slowly lifting to the softly vulnerable curve of her lips, the dreamy green of her eyes, and he said thickly, 'My God— I think I'm jealous of my own son!' And then he went on, taking in her fiery blush, 'When you took that job in France and told me you wanted a separation, I nearly went out of my mind. Things had been going badly for us—I knew how much you wanted children. I think, on the whole, that desire was responsible for turning the tide in my favour when you agreed to marry me.'

'You said you wanted children, too. Hordes of them, to fill South Park,' she reminded him defensively, and he held up a quietening hand.

'Only because I knew how keen you were. I wanted you, only you. If you gave me children, great. But if you hadn't been able to I wouldn't have gone into a decline, believe me,' he told her drily. 'And I believed seeing young Harry, in our home, was the final straw, the thing that sent you away. I'd been responsible—in my own mind at least—for the way you'd lost your baby. And, for all we knew, lost all hope of having any more. I tried to make you believe that there would be more for you—more to comfort you than to ease my own conscience. I could see how Harry's presence was hurting you, making you bitter. I hadn't been able to touch you, you see. Partly because of my feelings of guilt and partly because I knew if we shared the same bed I wouldn't be able to keep my hands off you. I felt you needed time to come to terms with what had happened, without my making that sort of demand.'

She had been thinking about his words, words about wanting her, and only her, allowing them to linger on her mind like soothing balm, and about him saying he'd tried to comfort her, telling her there would be more children for her when, at the time, she'd believed he'd meant men! But his statement about the effect his son had had on her jolted her out of the dangerous fool's paradise. Of course Harry's presence had hurt, made her bitter and jealous!

'I was hurt because Harry was—is—your son,' she told him tightly, feeling the ache of loneliness and loss build up inside her again. 'I heard Zanna call him "our son", say she'd had to come to you again because the boy needed to get to know his father. Tell you she'd heard our marriage was over, which it was to all intents and purposes—and only you could have told her that. And I saw you together that night, in the nursery, and Mrs Penny said Harry was the spitting image of you, which he is, and——'

'Mrs Penny always did know more than is good for her,' Charles interrupted, lifting a hand to gentle away the tears she hadn't been able to prevent escaping from beneath her closed eyelids. 'Don't upset yourself, my love. There really is no need. Because you do love me, don't you?'

The deep note of triumph in his voice made her shiver. And she nodded, too emotional now to speak, to even try to salvage the pride that had become so important to her.

He took the now sleeping baby from her arms and tucked him gently back in his cradle, then sat on the bed, pulling her into his arms, telling her huskily, 'I worked that out for myself, in between ministering to you while you were so gallantly producing our son and heir! From what you'd told me, I knew you couldn't have overheard all that conversation, as I'd believed. If you had, you would have known that Harry is James's son, not mine! You left because you believed Zanna had come back to me, bringing our son, and I was going to turn you out.'

'James's son?' Beth lifted her face from the haven of his broad chest, her eyes incredulous. 'But she was having an affair with you—everyone knew how obsessed you were with her.'

He dropped his mouth to her parted lips, whispering against them, 'I never had an affair with Zanna. And as for being obsessed, I suppose I was, in a way. Obsessed by the need to keep her away from James.'

An imperious rap on the door heralded the arrival of a nurse, ignoring the 'Do Not Disturb' notice which was for the benefit of visitors only.

'Has Baby been fed, Mrs Savage?' she asked briskly, and, at Beth's bemused nod, whisked him out of his comfortable nest. 'Then it's time he was changed, isn't it? You only had to press that bell.'

Watching the starched, retreating back, Beth shook her head bemusedly. Was she being accused of being an uncaring mother? She rather thought she was! But, instead of being justifiably indignant, she curved her mouth in a soft smile. Already she loved her tiny son more than life. But she loved his father even more, and it was beginning to make sense, some of it...

Had everyone been wrong about his tempestuous affair with the gorgeous redhead?

'Explain,' she commanded, drawing away from the arms which were still holding her so close.

'I'll have to, won't I?' His eyes gleamed with devilry. 'But all I can really take in is the fact that, after all the traumas, you love me.' His lips took hers, but gently, savouring her, the hint of tightly leashed, underlying passion making her head spin. And long, delicious minutes later, he cradled her head against his shoulder and told her, 'To go back years, our family have always known the Halls. Zanna's father and mine were at the same schools together. She was always a minx—lovely, granted, but totally uncontrollable. I found her more annoying than intriguing. And then, five years or so ago, she came to stay with us. Her parents were sick of her behaviour, the way she went through men. There were always broken-hearted ex-men-friends littering their doorstep, apparently. What they didn't know, though, was that James had been

secretly smitten for years. But I knew it, and maybe
I was being over-protective, but I didn't want to see
him go the way of all the others, so I took it on
myself to squire the woman around, letting James
think I was the current lover. Unfortunately...' He
ran his hands over her back, his fingers burning
through the thin silk of her nightgown, making her
melt against him. 'Everyone else believed it, too,'
he continued. 'It was the most misguided thing I'd
ever done in my life. It caused a rift between us,
James and me, and it's only recently been healed.
At the time, I believed I'd done the right thing,
especially when James, who had gone to work on
a project in France, married Lisa. Zanna was still
hanging around and, to be fair, she did make herself
useful, acting as my hostess when I needed her—
in between flitting hither and thither, doing her own
thing. Crunch time came when she told me she'd
visited James and Lisa—she actually had the gall
to tell me she'd fallen in love with him, that they'd
had an affair, practically under Lisa's nose.
Needless to say, I threw her out, told her never to
darken my doorstep again, et cetera. I think the
whole village believed the boot was well and truly
on the other foot, that she'd given me my marching
orders. Everyone, all of a sudden, became remarkably sympathetic!'

'She's hateful!' Beth exploded hotly.

Charles said drily, 'She can be. But I think she's
changed. She'll always be headstrong, always hog
the limelight, but she's a good mother—and that
surprised me—and she and James love each other.
If he can handle her temperament, they'll be OK.'

'So James really is Harry's father,' Beth whispered, hardly able to believe that at last everything was beginning to fall into place. 'And you thought I knew that all along, and wouldn't discuss it when you and she invited me to. I just walked out. You and Zanna must have thought me a prize bitch.'

'Never that, my love.' He smiled into her troubled eyes, lifted her hands and kissed both palms with a lingering tenderness that made her want to weep with the depth and the beauty of her love for him. 'I believed you were troubled, and hurt—that seeing young Harry had brought back all you had missed out on. And when you went I was determined to get you back. I knew my life wouldn't be worth living without you.'

'Then what were you doing with her in France?' Beth, with an effort, stopped herself from melting against him and gave him an angular look, and he shook his head, lifting his eyes.

'Patience, woman. I'm trying to tell you. We were going to find James. But the first I knew of Harry's existence was when Zanna turned up at South Park with him that day. She was putting a brave face on it—trying to be her old, flamboyant self—but boy was she worried underneath. She told me that Harry was my nephew and that, having heard of Lisa's untimely death, she needed to contact him but had no idea where he was. Harry had a right to get to know his father, and James, now free, might still care enough for her to marry her. She still loved him. Which, quite frankly, knowing her track record, I could hardly credit. Anyway——' he shrugged wide shoulders '—there was no doubt that the boy was James's; the family likeness was too strong to overlook. So I promised I'd do what I could. I knew he was still working with the same firm of civil engineers in France and managed to track him down to a small town in the south. But first I had to find you. As you know, I learned where you were from Allie, phoned James to warn him we were arriving—and when—and stopped off at Boulogne, much to Zanna's annoyance, because, having arranged that meeting with James, she hated the thought of delay.

'I found you and intended to talk things through with you, ask you to give me the opportunity to try again. But, as you know again, things got out of hand and the day I'd given myself to persuade you was over. But I knew where you were, knew you would stay put with that William guy, and what with helping to sort things out between James and Zanna, sorting out a few pressing business affairs of my own to give me the time to spend with you, hiring that cottage and stocking it, it was weeks before I could come for you again—knowing I'd have enough time, hopefully, to persuade you to my point of view.'

'Which is?' Beth prompted, resolutely pushing the misery of the last year out of her head, knowing that the present and the future she had with this one man was the only thing that mattered.

'To teach you to love me,' he answered simply. 'I'd loved you almost from the moment you came to South Park as my temporary housekeeper. You were so warm, so natural, so caring. I couldn't believe my good fortune when you agreed to marry me.'

'You didn't tell me you loved me,' Beth accused, but softly. She recalled how she'd ached to hear him say those words, but that was all behind her now, and nothing mattered because she knew the truth.

The surprise in his eyes made her want to shake him for being so cussedly male, but she kissed him instead when he told her, 'I showed you, didn't I? Every time I held you in my arms I showed you how much I loved you. And when I get you home, after a suitable interval for your recovery, of course, I'll show you again, and again . . .' He gathered her slowly into his arms and brushed his mouth against hers, invoking a response she should have been too exhausted to give, all things considered, she thought dizzily, and she twined her arms around his neck, intent on showing him how exhausted she was not, when he lifted his head and said,

'And before you ask, Zanna and James are back in England to break the news of their marriage to Lisa's parents. James thought it politic to go on ahead, with Harry, to break the ice as it were. Zanna came to South Park to beg a bed for the night. Even now she's on her way up north to join the others.'

'Blow Zanna!' Beth muttered hoarsely, pulling his head down to hers, and things were starting to get out of hand when the starchy nurse—so different from the fluttery blonde from the night before—announced stiffly,

'Baby thinks he needs feeding again, I do believe. He's been bathed and changed and weighed and——'

'Thank you.' Charles was on his feet, taking his wide-eyed, grumbling son into the crook of his arm, ushering the nurse on her way.

He drew Beth to her feet, his other arm around her, supporting and cherishing her, holding her close, and his voice was deep with emotion as he murmured, 'Can you feel it, Beth? The love that surrounds us? I swear there's enough of it here, in this room, to make the world go round for a thousand years.'

And she looked deep into those hard gunfighter's eyes, and saw love, and silently pledged her love to him for the rest of her life. And he understood— he read the message that was too deep to put into words and brushed his lips across hers as she took the protesting infant into her arms, settled him to her breast and held out her free hand to her husband, her wonderful, tough, soft-centred, exasperating Charles. And her smile was glorious.

Relive the romance...
Harlequin®is proud to bring you.

A new collection of three complete novels every
month. By the most requested authors, featuring
the most requested themes.

Available in October:

DREAMSCAPE

They're falling under a spell!
But is it love—or magic?

Three complete novels in one special collection:

GHOST OF A CHANCE by Jayne Ann Krentz
BEWITCHING HOUR by Anne Stuart
REMEMBER ME by Bobby Hutchinson

Available wherever Harlequin books are sold.

Calloway Corners

In September, Harlequin is proud to bring readers four involving, romantic stories about the Calloway sisters, set in Calloway Corners, Louisiana. Written by four of Harlequin's most popular and award-winning authors, you'll be enchanted by these sisters and the men they love!

MARIAH by Sandra Canfield
JO by Tracy Hughes
TESS by Katherine Burton
EDEN by Penny Richards

As an added bonus, you can enter a sweepstakes contest to win a trip to Calloway Corners, and meet all four authors. Watch for details in all Calloway Corners books in September.

CAL93

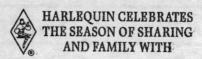

1993 Keepsake

Stories

Capture the spirit and romance of Christmas with KEEPSAKE CHRISTMAS STORIES, a collection of three stories by favorite historical authors. The perfect Christmas gift!

Don't miss these heartwarming stories, available in November wherever Harlequin books are sold:

ONCE UPON A CHRISTMAS by Curtiss Ann Matlock
A FAIRYTALE SEASON by Marianne Willman
TIDINGS OF JOY by Victoria Pade

ADD A TOUCH OF ROMANCE TO YOUR HOLIDAY SEASON WITH KEEPSAKE CHRISTMAS STORIES!

HX93

HARLEQUIN PRESENTS®

A Year DOWN UNDER

In 1993, Harlequin Presents celebrates the land down under. In October, let us take you to rural New Zealand in WINTER OF DREAMS by Susan Napier, Harlequin Presents #1595.

Olivia Marlow never wants to see Jordan Pendragon again—their first meeting had been a humiliating experience. The sexy New Zealander had rejected her then, but now he seems determined to pursue her. Olivia knows she must tread carefully—she has something to hide. But then, it's equally obvious that Jordan has his own secret....

Share the adventure—and the romance—of A Year Down Under!

Available this month in A YEAR DOWN UNDER

AND THEN CAME MORNING
by Daphne Clair
Harlequin Presents #1586
Available wherever Harlequin books are sold.